I0619443

PARANORMAL COZY MYSTERY

Dames & Deadly Games

TRIXIE SILVERTALE

Sittin' On A Goldmine
Productions L.L.C.

Copyright © 2021 by Trixie Silvertale

All rights reserved. Sittin' On A Goldmine Productions, L.L.C. and Trixie Silvertale reserve all rights to *Dames and Deadly Games, Mitzy Moon Mysteries 13*. No part of this work may be reproduced, uploaded, scanned, distributed, or transmitted in any form or by any manner whatsoever, or stored in a database or retrieval system, without the prior written permission of the publisher, except for the use of brief quotations in a book review. Please purchase only authorized editions and do not participate in or encourage piracy of copyrighted materials. Your support of the author's rights is appreciated.

MITZY MOON MYSTERIES and the "TEAL SEAL" design are trademarks belonging to Sittin' On A Goldmine Productions, L.L.C.

Sittin' On A Goldmine Productions, L.L.C.

pr@sittinonagoldmine.co

www.sittinonagoldmine.co

This is a work of fiction. Names, characters, places, and incidents are products of the author's imagination or are used fictitiously and are not to be construed as real. Any resemblance to actual events, locales, business establishments, organizations, or persons, living or dead, is entirely coincidental.

ISBN: 978-1-952739-04-0

Cover Design © Sittin' On A Goldmine Productions, L.L.C.

Trixie Silvertale
Dames and Deadly Games: Paranormal Cozy Mystery : a novel /
by Trixie Silvertale — 1st ed.

[1. Paranormal Cozy Mystery — Fiction. 2. Cozy Mystery — Fiction. 3. Amateur Sleuths — Fiction. 4. Female Sleuth — Fiction. 5. Wit and Humor — Fiction.] 1. Title.

THE STEADY MOTION of the train isn't comforting —it's claustrophobic. Something's not right. It's almost like a bad dream. Maybe it is a dream?

Like any good film-school dropout, I pinch myself. Assuming that old trope holds true, the resulting pain proves I'm awake. However, it's black as a moonless night.

Shouldn't some light seep under the door of the sleeping compartment?

My head throbs. I suppose I should've listened to Erick and taken it easy on the free champagne last night.

Wait. I can't extend my legs. There's no way I'm in a sleeping compartment.

A quick Marcel Marceau, mime-style check of

the perimeter confirms my worst fear: I'm inside some kind of trunk!

Panic crushes my chest in an iron grip.

I want to scream, but my lungs refuse to co-operate.

All the dangerous risks I've taken, and *this* is how I go out?

I could really go for one of Sheriff Erick Harper's warnings right about now.

CHAPTER 1

AT LAST! Spring has sprung! And it has nothing to do with the calendar. Trust me when I tell you that March came in like a lion and went out like a T-Rex. I mean, I'm walking down Main Street at a leisurely pace in my short-sleeved shirt in mid-April. A feat that would've bordered on life-threatening merely two weeks ago. The great lake nestled in Pin Cherry's harbor has finally relented. The ice floes have all but vanished, and the sun is busy sparkling off the crests of gentle waves as I approach my bookshop.

Where am I coming from, you ask?

It wouldn't be fair for me to spoil the surprise and tell you before I share the exciting news with my dearly departed grandmother.

Pulling my one-of-kind brass key from under

my shirt, I slip the triangle-shaped barrel into the lock nestled in the aged wood of the massive front door and twist three times.

Back in the old days, I would've started shouting for my benefactor, Ghost-ma, the second I set foot inside the Bell, Book & Candle. However, a long-standing feud with a gypsy has trapped my grandmother's ghost in a vintage amber pendant. Fortunately, she can still see and hear me, but she can no longer come swooshing at my beck and call.

Taking a moment to inhale my favorite scent of the worlds hidden within these precious pages, I carefully navigate my way over the "No Admittance" chain at the bottom of the wrought-iron spiral staircase and, despite my clumsiness, make it to the other side unscathed. A quick trot across the Rare Books Loft brings me to the clever candle-sconce handle that opens a secret bookcase door into my posh apartment.

"Grams? Grams, you're still in here, right?"

A reassuring voice echoes from the closet I've nicknamed *Sex and the City* meets *Confessions of a Shopaholic*.

"Right where you left me."

Now that she's unable to take corporeal form or freely move about the three-story bookshop and printing museum, she generally asks me to hang the pendant inside this altar to all things couture when

I leave the premises. I'm sure she'd prefer the jewel containing her nosy essence dangle around my neck 24-7, but a girl needs a little privacy.

"Oh, sweetie! I'm so glad you're back. I thought I was losing my mind. This must be what the inside of a coffin feels like!"

"I was only gone thirty minutes. You're going to have to work on your patience."

I can picture her putting a bejeweled fist on her designer-gown-clad hip as her voice takes a sassy twist. "Oh, really? And are you the pot or the kettle in this scenario, dear?"

"Rude, but fair." Pacing around the padded mahogany bench in the center of the closet, I'm nearly bursting at the seams with my salacious news.

"Spill the beans, Mitzy. I have nothing to look forward to these days except gossip. Dish!"

Striking a pose opposite the amulet that serves as Ghost-ma's prison, I point a single finger meaningfully toward my lips. "Just because you're living inside some jewelry now doesn't mean the rules have changed. If these lips aren't moving—"

"I know. I know. No thought-dropping. But a woman has limits. Please take my mind off my predicament for a few minutes and share your story."

Rubbing my hands together, I launch into my tale. "Erick has a friend—"

"Oh, how is Erick? Did he have that gorgeous blond hair slicked back with pomade this morning, or was there a little chunk of his bangs hanging loosely across his eye?"

Pushing my own naturally snow-white hair back from my forehead, I groan. "Um, I think I've mentioned that I'm not comfortable with you swooning over my boyfriend. So why don't you take a big otherworldly step back and give me some room to tell my story about Sheriff Too-Hot-To-Handle?"

Grams giggles and the sound warms and breaks my heart simultaneously. In the months before her capture in this terrible soul trap, she and I had fallen into a comfortable routine. She would swish and float about my apartment in her burgundy silk-and-tulle Marchesa burial gown, and I would bask in the newfound joy of family and a grandmother's love.

A soft sniffling sound emanates from the necklace. "Oh, Mitzy, I miss wrapping my ghostly arms around you."

"Please don't cry, Grams. If I was having trouble figuring out how to deliver an afterlife handkerchief to your ghost, I'm fresh out of ideas as to how to shove one inside that pendant. No crying. All right?"

Snuffle. Sniffle. "Whatever you say, dear. Now tell me what Erick said."

"Anyway, he has a friend who's launching a brand-new marketing campaign for the Scenic North-Country Railway."

"Oh, I do love the train!"

I'm powerless to stop my eyes from rolling. "Of course you do. The fact that you were married to two separate railroad tycoons seems proof enough. Now, may I finish my story sans interruption?"

She softly whispers, "I'm covering my mouth with my hand and nodding. But I know you can't see me."

"Copy that." After repeated interruptions, the urgency has somewhat drained from my news bulletin, and I flop onto the padded bench. "The new campaign is 'ride the rails in luxury.' They've completely revamped three of the sleeping cars and added an extra first-class dining car. They went overboard! Fine china, Baccarat crystal, silver, elegant linens in the sleeping cars . . . It's like stepping back in time. At least, that's what Erick said."

"It sounds absolutely divine, dear, but why are you so excited?"

"Oh, right. Erick's friend offered him two first-class tickets to the grand opening excursion. It's a murder-mystery adventure. A weekend getaway on the train, in first-class luxury, plus we get to solve a fun murder."

Grams laughs so hard she snorts. "I don't think I've ever heard anyone use the phrase 'fun murder' before, but I shouldn't be surprised. Do you mean a pretend murder, sweetheart?"

"Obviously. That's why it's fun, because it's not real. Anyway, Erick and I are finally going to have our getaway."

I can easily imagine Grams clapping her hands as she shouts. "How exciting! I'll tell you what to pack and you pile it on the bench."

"Slow down, Danica Patrick! It's not that kind of getaway. We've both had a lot of changes in our life recently, and we agreed to a 'no pressure, no expectations' weekend. So don't start packing just yet. I actually saved the best part for last."

She scoffs. "Hardly! The best part is that you and Erick are going to be spending an unsupervised night together—at last!"

"I think you'll find that we spent several unsupervised nights together when we went to Arizona, but don't get me distracted. It's going to be a magical weekend, because the murder-mystery game is 1920s-themed!"

The squeal that echoes from the amber stone is close to deafening. "Unbelievable! Well, you absolutely have to go as Sidney Mae. I don't care what character they assigned you, you call them and tell them you've already got your own character for this mystery."

"As luck would have it, Grams, Erick already did me that favor. My character is a 1920s flapper who is also a lounge singer. Of course, everyone's using their actual names to make it a little less confusing for the participants, but between you and me, I plan to channel Sidney Mae Jensen all weekend."

A moment of silence hangs between us as Grams and I reflect on my illustrious ancestor, whose vintage beaded dress adorns a mannequin under glass in my apartment. When I first arrived, I didn't pay it much mind. It was one of many fusty antiques decorating the premises. But after I met Sidney's ghost, the display came to hold a special place in my heart. She unfortunately died in a hail of mobster bullets in the 1920s while playing the saxophone at a speakeasy. Of course, if you think that sounds exactly like the kind of woman Grams and I would have in our family tree, you're not wrong.

"Well, you already have one outfit. You can easily wear that replica costume we had designed for you last year. But are you supposed to stay in character all weekend?"

"Erick's friend said that we're supposed to stay in character until the murder is solved."

Grams hoots. "Well, then they shouldn't have invited you two! Because obviously you'll have that murder solved the first night!" She chuckles proudly. "So I guess the one outfit will do!"

"Am I hearing you correctly, Myrtle Isadora? You're telling me that one outfit is enough?"

"Oh my goodness, this soul trap contraption is stealing my will to live. Of course one outfit isn't enough. You'll need sleepwear, a breakfast dress, something to wear to lunch, or for strolling through the passenger cars, and you absolutely must have a formal gown for the second evening's supper. I think I have something that can pass for 1920s couture . . ."

Lying back on the bench, I lace my fingers behind my head and listen to my fabulous grandmother plan my weekend's fashion. I can't say I'm looking forward to all the high heels she's sure to force into my suitcase, but I am absolutely bursting with excitement about having Erick all to myself for three whole days.

Fate is always getting in the way of our romantic endeavors. Trapped on a train, sharing a sleeping compartment . . . I can't think of anything more perfect.

I suppose I better figure out who's going to feed Pyewacket—

"RE-ow." Feed me.

As per usual, my half-wild caracal appears without assistance or warning. He drops majestically onto his tan behind and, while his large golden eyes fix me with reproach, his tufted black ears flick back and forth expectantly.

"I'm sure Twiggy will be more than happy to fill your bowl with your favorite Fruity Puffs while I'm away. But just in case she's too busy, I'll check with Silas as a backup."

My plans, plural, seem to pass muster. Pyewacket squeezes his eyes closed, and I chuckle at his indifference.

Sliding out my phone, I call my mentor and lawyer, and tap the speakerphone button in case Pye needs to add anything.

"Good morning, Mr. Willoughby. I hope you are having a lovely day."

Despite my careful use of the manners he holds so dearly, he harrumphs with displeasure before he replies. "I have not yet discovered a way of releasing your grandmother from the cursed amulet, while at the same time preventing her freed spirit from permanently crossing over. As I mentioned on several of your previous calls, I will contact you directly as soon as I uncover a fresh approach."

Ouch. Someone's a little cranky. To be fair, I have been calling him twice a day, every day, pressuring him for a magical—I mean, alchemical—solution to my grandmother's situation. "I'm sorry to drive you crazy with my phone calls. But the good news is today's request has nothing to do with Grams."

He clears his throat, and I can picture him smoothing his mustache with his thumb and forefinger. "Ah, a welcome respite. Do tell."

"I'm gonna be gone for the weekend, and I was wondering if I could count on you to stop in once on Saturday and once on Sunday to feed Mr. Cuddlekins?"

Silas laughs with far more enthusiasm than I expect. "I had forgotten your grandmother's absurd nickname for such a magnificent beast. It would be my pleasure to act as valet for his royal furriness while you are away. There are several tomes in your erudite collection that deserve another perusal."

"Thanks, I think. The place is all yours. I'll be leaving this afternoon, around 3:00 p.m."

"Are you planning another journey to your birthplace in Arizona?"

"No way. Going back there to solve my mother's suspicious death was enough for me. If I never see the dry riverbeds and prickly cactus of the Southwest again, I can't say I'll be disappointed.

But, now that you mention the cringey ol' days, it makes me wonder about something."

"Well, don't keep me in suspense, Mizithra. What is it that you ponder?"

"When you knocked on my door that day, in that sketchy rundown apartment building, what did you think when I opened the door? You know, first impression stuff."

He chuckles again, but there's a warmth and caring buried in the humor. "As I traveled toward Sedona, I had a great deal of time to reflect upon what I would encounter. I suppose I toyed with the fanciful notion that you would be elegant and privileged. Your grandmother's stately bearing always struck me as something that would be passed down."

Laughter grips me before I have a chance to stifle it. "I must've scared the bejeezus out of you!"

"Truth be told, the minute I saw your intelligent grey eyes and that unmistakable ghost-white hair, I knew you were a force to be reckoned with. Of course, you did not have the trappings of wealth, but you had the Duncan fire. Regardless of the torments life had thrown at you, by stealing your mother when you were a young girl and tossing you into the foster system like so much human debris, your spirit remained unbroken. On that day, I was unsure whether you would risk a journey north to

Pin Cherry Harbor and examine your grandmother's bequest, or whether you would perhaps waste all the money at a seedy pub. But let me be the first to tell you, I am immensely pleased with the decision you made. Your burgeoning psychic gifts are a pleasure to behold, and each day you spend with us reminds me why I chose to mentor you."

By the time he finishes his heartwarming soliloquy, both Grams and I are in tears. "For crying out loud, Silas. You sure know how to hit a girl where it hurts."

He harrumphs loudly. "I should think you would take my words as a compliment, not an affront."

"I did, I mean, I do. That's why I'm crying. Everything you've done for me since I came here . . . I can never repay you."

He adopts a stern fatherly tone as he replies. "If your weekend adventure is in the company of Sheriff Harper, then you can repay me by forgetting all about your responsibilities at the bookshop for a few days. That principled man deserves your undivided attention, for once in his life."

"Copy that."

We all chuckle, and Pye even tosses me a wink.

Swiping away my happy tears, I jump to my feet. "All right. I have to get packed. Do you want to meet me at the diner for lunch?"

"Regrettably, I have a video call scheduled with my brother at noontime."

You could pick my jaw up off the floor with a forklift. "You have a brother?"

"Indeed. Surely I've spoken of him before?"

"I'm sure you have not. You having a brother is not something I'd forget. Trust me."

Silas makes no reply.

"Is he older or younger? Is he married? Does he have kids? Does he ever visit you? Does he like cats? Is he an alchemist, too?"

Silas clicks his tongue, and I imagine his head shaking in dismay. "I believe it would be prudent for you to focus on your packing. We can discuss the branches of my family tree when you return from your trip. Where is Mr. Harper taking you?"

"Oh, right." I smack myself playfully on the forehead with the palm of my hand. "On the train! We're taking a scenic train trip along the great lakes and we get to play in a murder-mystery game. It's going to be off the chain."

"I will assume that indicates an enjoyable excursion for all."

"You assume correctly."

"Very well. Enjoy your trip and do not give Pyewacket a second thought. He will be well cared for in your absence."

My thumb hovers over the end button, when a

sudden thought intrudes. "Oh, and don't forget to come into the closet and talk to Grams. I know she can't write out messages to you anymore, but she'll feel better if she can hear a human voice at least once before I get back."

Grams sighs with relief. "Oh, thank you, dear. I'm sure I would go absolutely mad if I had to hang here in silence for three days."

"It's only two-and-a-half days, Grams."

Silas can only hear my side of the conversation, but that part is enough to cause laughter. "I shall do my best to entertain your jewelry."

"That's a good man."

I end the call and retrieve a medium-size suitcase and a small overnight bag from the cupboard under the stairs. The only thing I currently have in my favor is that Grams can't secretly slip any lingerie into my suitcase when I'm not looking.

"Don't underestimate my power over Pyewacket, young lady."

"Oh brother."

CHAPTER 2

TIME IS SLIPPING AWAY FASTER than the sands through a wicked witch's hourglass. Erick will pick me up in less than an hour, and Grams and I have only agreed on two outfits. Just when I think things can't get any worse—

"Reeeee-ow." A warning.

Storming out of the closet, I place my hands on my hips and prepare to reprimand Pyewacket. However, when I catch sight of his forlorn expression as he sprawls in front of the camera and microphone set up I installed for Phoom calls before my last extended getaway, I can't bring myself to be upset. Walking toward him, I scratch firmly between his ears. "What's wrong, big guy? I'm barely gonna be gone two days. You hardly notice me when I'm here. I'm sure you'll be fine."

He rolls onto his back and swats playfully at my hand with one of his large paws. And I can assure you it's playful, because he keeps his deadly claws retracted.

As I try to pull my hand away, he curves his paw around my wrist and a hint of needle-sharp warning presses into my skin.

"Easy! Give me a minute to access my extrasensory perceptions." I take a deep breath and focus on the tan tyrant. My hand is already conveniently pressed against his chest, so it's simple to let my clairsentience lead the way. Let's see, it's not fear. He's not afraid to be alone. No surprise there. Oh, poor thing! He feels left out. "Are you worried that I won't be able to solve the pretend murder on the train without your helpful clues?"

"Reow." Can confirm.

With my free hand, I gently stroke his broad head between his lovely tufted ears. "Trust me, Mr. Cuddlekins, if it were a real murder, I'd be packing you in my suitcase. I can handle a little playacting. Besides, you have to stay home and keep Grams company." Leaning down toward his intelligent eyes, I wink and whisper softly, "You have to protect what little is left of her sanity."

Clearly my voice wasn't quiet enough.

"Well, I never!" she exclaims from the closet.

"I think we both know that's not true, Myrtle

Isadora Johnson Linder Duncan Willamet Rogers."
We share a giggle at the laundry list of her former
husbands, but Pyewacket has still not released my
hand.

"Fine. Let's run a test of the Phoom system, just
in case I need to call for help to solve a fake
homicide."

A grumbling purr vibrates the wildcat's chest,
and he releases my hand.

It's been a few months since I've used the system, and it takes me a minute to remember the
proper settings. But I'll use my psychic powers to
replay the memory of the quick training session if
necessary. In fact, I would do just about anything to
avoid having to call the Northland's one and only
IT specialist. Yes, he was a friend of Erick's in high
school and one of the only people besides Erick's
mother who still refers to him as Ricky, but I don't
have time for big personalities or computer glitches
in my current schedule.

"All right, Pye, I think I've got everything set up
properly. I'm going to call you. Do you remember
what to do?"

Pyewacket drops into the chair, spins around
and places both of his front paws on the desk, like
it's his job. I can't help but snicker. "Here goes." I
tap "Headquarters" on my favorites list and wait as
the call goes through. The blinking light and a

buzzer jump to life on the videoconferencing system.

Pyewacket calmly shifts his weight onto the desktop and with his right paw smacks the green button on the screen.

The system springs to life, and I see an image of myself holding my phone in my apartment pop up on the screen. Pyewacket leans forward and presses his head against the screen.

"Congratulations, son. You got mad computer skills. Maybe I should put you to work downstairs helping Twiggy with inventory."

A moment later, my stubborn caracal reaches out with his right paw and ends the call.

Wow, I guess he really does know what he's doing. Now that his little kitty-cat tantrum is over, I have to finish packing my suitcase—and make sure I have a toothbrush.

Grams and I bicker over a few more outfits, and in the end I don't have the strength to protest. I pack everything she tells me, including four pairs of shoes! Which I'm obviously not going to wear in two days!

"You never know what the occasion might call for."

Yeesh! I zip the rolling suitcase closed and trundle it toward the door. Grabbing the overnight case, I hustle into the bathroom and throw everything on the counter in the bag. That should cover it!

BING. BONG. BING.

"He's here!" Despite her current residence inside a gemstone, Grams yells right along with me, as if on cue.

Taking my overnight case with me, I unhook the chain at the bottom of the wrought-iron circular staircase and tiptoe toward the entrance facing the alley.

"You better hook that back up, doll. You don't want to set off the alarm." My volunteer employee, Twiggy, admonishes me from the back room.

"Can you deactivate it? Erick needs to come in and carry down my big suitcase. I don't want him fiddling around with that stupid chain. You can hook it up and reactivate the alarm when I'm gone."

Twiggy's cackle echoes toward me as I hurry to the side door where the service bell is located. "You got it, kid. I'd hate to be the reason you trip and fall. Not that you won't find another way, but at least I can take that option off the table." She continues to enjoy a hearty laugh at my expense, which is the only form of payment she receives for her help at the bookshop. She and my grandmother had an understanding, and somewhere inside that tough exterior she likes me enough to fold me into it as well.

Opening the back door, I set my overnight bag

down and smile up at Sheriff Harper. "You're just in time. Did you find everything you needed at the thrift store?"

He pretends to be very confused and taps one sexy finger on his full, kissable lips. "If that's the only bag you're bringing on this trip, I'll eat my spats."

The laughter that grips me makes standing upright difficult. Even though I could manage, I'd rather purposely fall into his arms. "You better get used to taking care of dainty little me. I understand fainting was far more common at the turn of the century."

He smiles and kisses me lightly. Before he leans me back onto my own two feet, I soak in a breath of his woodsy-citrus scent.

"Is your other suitcase up in the apartment?"

I open my eyes as though I'm shocked, but nod in the affirmative. "Are you excited to be a gangster?"

A grin turns up the corner of my mouth as he strides ahead of me toward the stairs, shaking his head with laughter. "I think it will be fun to play the character of a gangster as part of this murder mystery. For the record, I have never been, nor will I ever be, an actual gangster."

"Copy that, Sheriff."

He smirks and takes the stairs two at a time.

He's back in a flash with my large suitcase and a feline escort blocking his descent. "Are you seeing this, Mitzy? If I didn't know better, I'd think the cat's trying to tag along."

"He probably is. He's worried I won't be able to solve the case without him."

Erick leans down and scratches Pyewacket between the ears. To my surprise, the furry beast allows the affection and even seems to lean into it a little. "Don't worry, Pyewacket, I'll take good care of her. And I'll try to be of as much assistance as you."

Pye makes a rough sound that could easily be mistaken for a scoff, and rockets down the stairs and into the stacks.

Erick brings the suitcase, hooks the chain up, and before we make it two steps from the bottom of the stairs—

"Thanks, Sheriff," Twiggy calls from the back room.

"Not a problem, Twiggy. I know how important security is around here. Job number one, right?"

"10-4," she replies.

He continues out the side door to load my luggage, and I pause to give Twiggy a final update. "I'll be back Sunday night. Silas said he'll stop by on Saturday and Sunday to feed the cat. But if you're going to be here, you can always call him off."

She shakes her grey pixie cut and taps the toe of

one biker boot. "Nah. I haven't seen that old fart in a month of Sundays. It'll be nice to catch up."

"All right. Wish me luck."

She slowly rotates away from the computer screen, toward me, in her dilapidated rolly office chair, and a faint smirk tugs at the corner of her mouth. "Luck? You already got all those special powers and you can see ghosts, for crying out loud. How much more luck does one girl need?"

"Accurate." Taking a comic bow, I offer her a final wave and head out to the waiting car.

Standing in the alley next to Erick's 1968 copper-brown Chevy Nova SS, I smile when he leans into the trunk to arrange my suitcase. Grams is right. The man knows how to fill out a pair of jeans. "Remind me again why we can't take the squad car?" I ask questions I don't really want to know the answer to when I need to distract myself.

He slams the trunk and rests one hand on the car. "I'm all for deputies driving their patrol cars home. Statistics show they take better care of the vehicles when they feel a sense of ownership, and the presence in neighborhoods acts as a crime deterrent. I'm just not crazy about the idea of leaving a sheriff's vehicle in an unsecured parking lot for three days. The train depot isn't in the best part of town, you know."

"I'll have you know, my father owns a railroad!" I shove my fists on my hips in feigned indignation.

"Nice try, Moon. You know as well as I do that the scenic train isn't part of the Midwest Union Railroad and it doesn't depart from your father's depot."

I smirk and roll my eyes. "So you think some local hooligans might get up to no good if they saw the opportunity to deface a piece of county property?"

Erick saunters toward me and slips an arm around my waist. "Let's just say I'd rather keep my focus on the important things this weekend and not get distracted with worry about a parked patrol car."

Tingles. Wobbly knees. Surges of warmth adding a pinkish hue to my cheeks. "Mmhmm."

He kisses me teasingly on the cheek and opens the car door for me.

As usual, the Nova brings out his inner rebel and he burns rubber out of the alley.

Once we're officially underway, I discover that it's a forty-five-minute drive to the North-Country Railway depot. "Looks like we have some time on our hands. Why don't you tell me when you got the nickname Ricky?"

He shakes his head, and an adorable swath of his long bangs falls loosely over one eye. "My mother is one hundred percent to blame for that.

Ever since I was little, she called me Ricky. Once friends started coming over to the house to hang out, they naturally repeated what they heard. Back in the day, the only people who called me Erick were teachers, coaches, and occasionally the principal."

A run-in with his principal? This is all new to me. Leaning eagerly toward the driver's seat, I whisper, "Go on."

He shakes his head. "It's not a very interesting story. The one and only time I tried to be a bad boy in high school, I was the guy who got caught and ended up taking the punishment for the whole crew, because I refused to narc."

I nod my head in approval. "Good job. Bros before hoes and all that, right?"

He chokes on his laughter. "That's not exactly how I would put it, but yeah. I thought it would be best to take my lumps and protect the rest of the guys."

"So what did you and the guys get up to?"

He clenches his jaw briefly, and I can sense him struggle with letting down his guard. "It was a senior prank kind of thing. Every year the outgoing senior class pulls some kind of amazing prank and raises the bar for the junior class. I got some unsavory ideas from my uncle, and when I shared them with the group, everyone thought they were fantastic."

"What was this uncle's genius plan?"

"Supposedly, if you take a raw chicken leg and put it in a mason jar full of milk, and screw the lid on, but not too tightly, the gas from the terrible experiment will eventually blow the lid off and fill whatever space you've left it in with the horrible odor of rotting flesh. My uncle told me it was a surefire way to get away with a prank, because it wouldn't deliver until after graduation. He figured that by the time everyone came back to school in the fall, the entire school would have to be shut down for a HAZMAT-style cleaning."

"Erick Harper! That is scandalous. I can't believe you were on board with this."

He shakes his head. "I know. I know. Youthful indiscretion and all that. However, spoiler alert, the janitor caught me placing the jar up into the ceiling behind one of the acoustic panels and dragged me to the principal's office by my ear."

I have to clutch my stomach to prevent bursting from laughter. "Oh, man. That's the difference between you and me—I almost never got caught. That's how I ended up being such a bad seed. If something like that had happened to me the first time . . . Well, we might not be having this conversation."

Erick's hand shoots over to my knee and he squeezes my leg firmly. "Then, despite my current profession, I guess I'm glad you were a juvenile delinquent."

"Yeah, me too." I lay my hand on top of his large, strong one and a lovely feeling of warmth and acceptance fills my chest. How did I get so lucky? I suppose it's best not to tempt fate with questions. "So, tell me what you managed to throw together for your 1920s gangster wardrobe."

He places both hands back on the steering wheel and chews on his lower lip. "I found a pin-stripe suit at the thrift store, and a pretty decent black fedora. I had a few dress shirts at home, and a tuxedo. My mom said I definitely needed a tuxedo for the second night's supper."

Leaning across the car, I put a hand on his shoulder and laugh conspiratorially. "Grams said the same thing when she forced me to pack a ball gown!"

"So she's still trapped in that necklace?"

"Yeah. It's really depressing if I think about it too much. I'm sincerely hoping we can find a way to get her out of there, but I don't want her spirit to cross over. You know?"

He nods. "Yeah, I guess that would be hard for you. You've gotten really close with her ghost since you came to town, right?"

"I know it's weird to talk about ghosts. Why do you think I waited so long to tell you? But yeah, Grams and I are super close. Even though she can't follow me around the bookshop or give me ghost hugs, having her in my life is important to me."

"I understand." A half smile curves his full lips.

It's a strange feeling to be talking openly about seeing and communicating with ghosts, but it's an important step in our relationship.

"Okay, back to wardrobe stuff. The rest of the bits and pieces I grabbed out of this old costume trunk in the garage. I swear, my mom kept every costume I've ever worn."

I smile and hug my arms around myself. "I knew there was a reason I liked your mother."

He chuckles. "I can assure you, the feeling is mutual. She asks about you almost every day. She forces me to repeat the tales of your amazing crime solving, and she constantly makes me promise to treat you right."

Tilting my head, I gaze into his deep-blue eyes. "Please let her know that she has an official fan club."

He scoffs and shakes his head. "My plan is to keep the two of you apart as long as possible."

"Rude."

Taking liberties with a move I invented, he walks his fingers across the center console and turns up his palm. I place my hand in his, and we drive connected, but in silence, for possibly ten whole minutes.

Erick clears his throat and fidgets in his seat. "Hey, I wanted to let you know about the sleeping arrangements, so there won't be any surprises."

"I'm all ears, Sheriff."

"The couple that canceled at the last minute had only booked one sleeper car. And the train is full. So we'll be sharing a sleeper car, if that's all right. If not, I'm happy to grab a reclining seat in one of the passenger cars."

"Reclining seat? Not happening. It's fine. There's no way I'm gonna make you sleep in a crummy seat while I bask in all the luxury of the sleeping compartment."

He nods and swallows loudly. "There are two sleeping berths."

"Of course there are." I can barely stifle my chuckle. "What's the bathroom situation?"

His sweet face scrunches up. "That's the other tricky bit. These are authentic 1920s cars that have been fully refurbished, but they're still historically accurate. So, there's a washstand cupboard with mirrors, hot and cold running water, and a sink. There are shower enclosures at either end of each sleeper car, as well as water closets."

"Ew. We have to share a bathroom with everyone else on the train?"

Erick shakes his head rapidly. "There are only four sleeping compartments per car. So at the most, that'll be eight people sharing two bathrooms."

"Hey, I'm sure for a guy who did two tours in Afghanistan, that sounds like the lap of luxury, but it's going to take me some getting used to."

He laughs. "Yeah, I guess that is slumming it for a wealthy heiress, eh?"

Ignoring his comment, I let my mind wander. The visual details of his explanation begin to construct a virtual sleeping compartment in my mind. "Wait, so if there's no bathroom in the compartment, where do I get changed?"

The hungry look that flashes across his face makes my tummy flip-flop. "I can step out when you want to change. Whatever you need. We'll figure it out." His hand is gripping the steering wheel so hard his knuckles are turning white, and my psychic senses are picking up on all kinds of little heartthrob-y red flags.

Eager to stir the pot, I toss a little gasoline on the fire. "I hope I remembered to pack some pajamas."

His carefully crafted composure nearly crumbles. "Yeah. That'd be good." His voice goes up an octave and he struggles to swallow.

CHAPTER 3

THE PARKING LOT at the Scenic North-Country Railway is bursting at the seams. I guess the sleeper cars aren't the only things that sold out. The coach-class passenger cars must be fully booked as well.

Erick insists on managing all our luggage, and I strut along beside him, ignoring the jealous glances tossed my way by other female passengers lugging various-size bags.

As we approach the depot, a lively tune ripples through the gathering throng. Turns out there's a jazz trio set up at the entrance in full 1920s attire. There's a standing base, a cornet, and a saxophone player. The shiny brass instrument brings instant memories of my ancestor to mind.

Sidney Mae Jensen, known as Sid Jensen. Grams told me she chose that nickname because people assumed it was a man's name, and it got her more gigs. She was the first female jazz saxophone player in the country—maybe the world. I never got the exact data, but she was incredibly famous. I had the opportunity to make her ghost's acquaintance last All Hallows Eve, but that's another story. I'm looking forward to adding some of her moxie to my character.

Inside the depot, Erick guides me toward the first-class passenger check-in. Once we pick up our tickets from will call, we head out to the platform and are greeted by a full staff. There's a conductor in a vintage uniform, as well as male and female porters ready to take our luggage to our compartment.

Passengers and staff alike are in high spirits. This maiden excursion of the refurbished railcars has garnered audience anticipation as well as media attention. Cameras are flashing, and two field reporters from, I'm assuming, rival channels record sound bites at opposite ends of the enclosed wooden platform.

Erick and I duck our heads to avoid appearing in any of the local rags and board the train behind our valet.

Despite the historic nature of the cars, everything smells crisp and new. The floor-to-ceiling inlaid wooden panels, with their multiple coats of lacquer, glisten in the late afternoon sun. Brass handles and railings are polished to a superior sheen, and the beautiful dark-red carpets have been vacuumed within an inch of their life. The porter stops, retrieves a key from his pocket, and opens our compartment. He takes the suitcases inside and gives us a tour.

Tour is a generous word, for a space measuring barely eight feet by ten feet.

He demonstrates how the corner washstand cupboard operates, as though we might not have knowledge of modern plumbing, and he informs us that our sleeping berths will be made up during the supper hour.

"If you have any valuables, there is a safe in the baggage car, and only the conductor possesses that key. If you need such accommodations, please let me know, and I'll send the conductor to your compartment. If you wish to stow your bags, I can take them to the baggage car at your request." He hands over a tagged key for our compartment.

Erick takes the key and gives the young man a ten-dollar bill and a warm smile. "Thank you. We're all set."

The steward steps into the hallway and gestures like a flight attendant to both ends of our car. "There is a shower and a water closet at either end.

You'll also find water closets at either end of the two restaurant cars."

He has my attention. "There's more than one restaurant?"

"There's a dining car for the open-seating passengers, as well as the modern addition of a bar car, also available to all passengers. However, only first-class passengers have access to the two restaurant cars. There's a small guidebook in the pocket by your window, should you wish to see the menus in advance. I'll stop by later to collect your reservation information for the weekend. You may choose to try both restaurants, before you make all your meal plans." He bows slightly and scoots off down the narrow passageway.

My bunkmate closes the door and looks at me in a way that makes most, if not all, of my skin tingle. Erick scoops me into his arms and kisses me extravagantly. "Let the games begin."

As my knees weaken beneath me, I'm very pleased with how tightly he's holding me. "Should we change into our costumes?" In my mind, I've cleverly concealed my eagerness with a monotone voice. His grin suggests otherwise.

"Let's wait until we're underway, and then I'll go check for a concierge or someone with a rundown."

"Copy that. What time do we depart?"

He checks his watch. "In about fifteen minutes. Can I get you any—?"

A soft knock at our door interrupts his offer.

"Come in."

A tiny dark-haired server in a plain 1920s lady's maid uniform carefully opens the door and bobs her head. "Would either of you care for champagne or an apéritif?"

Glancing at Erick, I flash my eyebrows and wink. "I'd love some champagne. In fact, we both would."

She nods and closes the door.

"I could get used to this, Sheriff."

"Take it easy on the booze, Moon. Don't forget you're here to solve a pretend murder."

I brush his objections away with a swipe of my hand and a scoff. "Come on, you and I are going to be able to solve this murder with our eyes closed and one hand each tied behind our backs. A little champagne will just grease the wheels."

He laughs and pulls me onto the beautifully upholstered brocade bench seat. "I can't believe I have you all to myself."

A fresh set of tingles wash over me as I lean toward him. "Ditto."

Another soft knock precedes the delivery of our crystal champagne flutes, and it's not long before we hear the departure announcement.

"All aboard!" The train's whistle toots three short blasts, and a final flurry of activity races across the platform.

At last, the steam engine springs to life, and a cloud of smoke signals the train is underway.

The comforting clackety-whir, clackety-whir, clackety-whir of the rails and the champagne lull me into a glorious stupor.

Erick slides his arm out from behind me and offers the stuffed bolster as his substitute.

"I'll go get the schedule of events, and two bottles of water. Sound good?"

I smile dreamily. "Mmhmm."

In his absence, the couple in one of the adjacent compartments has quite a disagreement. Raised voices, banging doors, or possibly suitcases, and eventually one of the two exits the compartment with an unnecessary door slam.

Great. I hope the soothing motion of the train and perhaps a drink at dinner will simmer those two down. I'm not "all aboard" with some other couple's drama keeping me up at night.

The next thing I remember is being startled awake when the door opens and Erick waves a small program in my face.

"What? Wait . . . Did I fall asleep?"

Chuckling, he scoots up next to me on the bench. "That champagne went straight to your head." He shares the paper with me and points out some highlights. "Before tonight's dinner, there's a mixer in the bar car. All the first-class passengers who are participating in the murder-mystery game will be there. We'll have a chance to meet the others, engage in small talk, and make our initial assessments before the lights go out and the murder is committed."

I slide the paper from his hand and peruse the punch list. "Somehow, knowing exactly when the murder is going to happen takes a little of the fun out of it."

Erick shakes his head. "I don't think murders are supposed to be fun, Moon."

"You're the second person to say that to me today." I shrug and change the topic. "Should we scope out the train before we get changed?"

He blushes and looks away. "Why don't I make our dinner reservations while you get into costume?"

"Sounds good. I'll text you when I'm decent." There, that sounded completely composed. No vocal indication of my rising anxiety or anticipation.

He grins and nuzzles my neck. "Or before . . ."

Oops, there goes my calm exterior! "Erick Harper! Mind your manners."

Laughing, he heads to the door. "Just so you know, cell reception will be spotty soon, and there

are going to be long stretches where there's no service at all."

"What? No cell service?"

"Yep. The line runs in and out of Canadian ter-
ritory, and down some steep-walled canyons. The
cell towers just don't reach it."

I'm still nodding absently as he leaves the compartment. Shoot! I might not be able to check in
with Pyewacket. I sure hope Silas spends as much
time as he planned at the bookstore. I'd hate to
think what kind of damage my spoiled feline could
do if left unsupervised for too long. Too late to
worry about that now, I suppose.

Opening the washstand doors, I admire the polished brass fixtures and marble basin while I unload
my overnight case as neatly as possible, and set my
larger suitcase on the bench seat.

There's a small closet tucked cleverly behind
the door to our compartment. I hadn't even noticed
it earlier. Time to hang up my ball gown and a
couple more items that I don't want to wrinkle. The
beautiful red and silver flapper dress that I'll be
wearing this evening brings a tear to my eye. "This
one's for you, Sidney. I hope I can do the family
name justice."

Attempting a grown-up hairdo without the otherworldly aid of my grandmother is next to impossible. There's absolutely no time for elaborate finger

waves! So, I try to brush my hair into something bob-adjacent, and slip on my diamond-encrusted headband with its ruby accent stone and black and red ostrich feather plume, before any unruly strands can protest.

"There. That's kind of flapper-ish."

A quick application of kohl liner around my eyes and a swipe of bright-red lipstick finish the look.

Grams insisted I pack the proper decade's undergarments, and she claimed the dress requires a silk slip as well. So I have those layers on and I'm rolling up my stockings in preparation of clipping them into the garter belt when the door of the cabin opens.

Erick has a hand half covering his eyes. "I'm not looking, I promise." He slips in and quickly closes the door behind himself. "I had no service on my phone, so I wasn't sure if you had tried to text."

I pause my garter hooking operation, with one foot still balanced on the bench seat, and shake my head. "No service, huh? Isn't that convenient? As you can see—and trust me, I can tell you're peeking —I'm not dressed."

He continues to use his hand as a pathetically inadequate shield. "Are you decent? If you're decent, I can get dressed real quick. You won't even know I'm here. Trust me, after you've been through boot camp, modesty is kind of a thing of the past."

Attempting to walk the razor's edge between being a modern woman and taking our relationship slowly proves difficult. "I'm decent enough. Go ahead and get dressed."

He slowly drops his hand as the corners of his mouth curve up invitingly. "I'd say I got here just in time."

"Ha ha. Don't mind me, Sheriff. You focus on getting yourself ready."

He turns toward his suitcase, but his eyes are the last thing to peel away.

I hastily hook my other stocking and retrieve my intricately beaded, *Great Gatsby* eat-your-heart-out flapper dress from the closet.

The outer layer is a filmy sheath embellished with hundreds and hundreds of Swarovski crystals terminating in a fabulous red-beaded fringe. The red-and-silver theme catches the light from our personal chandelier.

I'm up to my ears in beads and silk when a soft voice whispers, "Do you need some help?"

"No." Sigh. "Yes! I don't know. It feels like it's caught on something."

I can feel him close the distance between us and reach his hands toward my gown.

Goosebumps parade down my arms as his fingers brush against my slip and tug on my dress. "There. Not stuck anymore."

My face is a shade of scarlet that certainly matches my dress. "It was the hips, wasn't it? The whole contraption was stuck on these darn bodacious hips!"

Erick hooks the clasp on the back of the ensemble and spins me to face him. "No complaints here. You look stunning. Those other passengers are going to be so shell-shocked when they catch sight of you, they'll forget all about solving the mystery."

Chuckling warmly, I lift on my tiptoes and kiss him. "Thank you. Thank you for always making me feel beautiful, even when I doubt myself."

He looks down at his feet and steps back. "Yeah, you should stop doing that. I wish you believed how amazing you are."

"Keep saying things like that, and I'm sure I'll join the fan club sooner or later."

He appraises me from head to toe and nods. "I better hurry up. Do you need help with your shoes?"

"Let me see if I can sit down in this dress, and then I'll let you know."

The fringe rocks back and forth against my thighs as I retrieve my shoes. Luckily, I'm able to sit somewhat comfortably, which allows me to reach the delicate hooks on my vintage red-satin T-straps.

Hands down the most comfortable heels Grams has ever foisted upon me.

Erick whips off his shirt, and, no matter how many times I take a gander, those abs never fail to steal my breath away.

He must feel my gaze on his skin. "Can I help you?" His hands are on his belt buckle and his eyes flicker with mischief.

All the saliva vanishes from my mouth and words escape me. I shake my head helplessly and rip my eyeballs away.

His throaty chuckle sends my tummy tumbling.

Focusing on my accessories is my only hope. I drape a beautiful red ostrich-feather boa over my left shoulder and knot an enormous strand of pearls around my neck, so they don't slip off.

I can see his reflection in the washstand mirror, but I force myself to straighten my cosmetics and fuss with my ruby teardrop earrings.

Erick is finally dressed and carefully buttoning his white spats over his black dress shoes when I catch sight of a fat cigar poking out of his bag. "You smoke?"

His big blue eyes pop open wide, and he shakes his head. "Not since the Army, and that was only to get actual breaks. When the sergeant says, 'Smoke 'em if you got 'em,' you figure out how to get 'em. If you don't, you're just asking for extra duties. Why do you ask?"

I point mutely to the cigar.

"Oh, that. I thought it was a good prop. It's probably too on the nose, but gangsters and cigars always go hand in hand in my mind."

"Understood."

He places his fedora at a rakish angle and offers me his elbow. "You ready to mix it up, doll?"

His crack at tough-guy vernacular tickles my funny bone something fierce, and I attempt to meet his character with a bold dame of my own. "I thought you'd never ask, big boy."

He gasps a little as I slip my arm through his elbow.

"What? Too much? I was just following your lead, Sheriff. I mean, Harper. I suppose I can't really call you sheriff anymore tonight, can I?"

"Nope. Better stick with Harper. But I like your moxie."

My eyes roll painfully. "Oh brother."

CHAPTER 4

THE WARMLY LIT passageway outside sleeper compartment 3C is too narrow for my mobster and me to walk arm in arm.

Erick extends a gentlemanly hand and allows me to lead the way to the bar car where the murder-mystery mixer will take place.

A delicate red velvet rope hangs below a gilt-edged sign announcing: "Bar Car closed for private event."

Mobster Harper unhooks the sash, and I strut in using all my psychic powers to channel my saucy ancestor.

A waiter in a white waistcoat approaches with a tray of champagne-filled coupe glasses, elegantly etched with a floral pattern.

"I believe I will have a glass of bubbles, mister."

I slip my fingers around the delicate stem and giggle.

Erick takes a glass and offers the waiter a silent nod. "You better take it easy on those, Moon. Remember, we're here to solve a crime, not make a scene."

Fully embracing my character, I kick out a hip and let my fringed beads wiggle as I lick my lip and smile. "I like to make a scene everywhere I go, tough guy. It ain't a scene unless you're seen."

He laughs. "To Mitzy Moon! The sexiest flapper on the Scenic Railway."

"I'll drink to that." We clink our glasses and he takes a sip of his champagne, while I down my entire glass, despite the bubbles tickling my nose. Before he can protest, I scoop another coupe from a passing tray. "Let's make the rounds, Harper. I want to check out the other movers and shakers."

We part company, to work the room and feel out the competition. I do love to watch that man walk away.

Taking a deep breath and a sip of champagne, for courage, I approach a stodgy old broad dressed to the nines, and her demure nurse. "How do you do? Mitzy Moon."

The woman adjusts her massive diamond brooch and clears her throat—twice. "Dame Joanna

Hecht. Tonight I'm to play a dowager, but I actually own this entire operation."

"Pleased to meet you. What—" As though I'm invisible, she cuts me off, and I'm left to drown in the aroma of her heavy floral perfume.

"That young couple over there just got married, but if you ask me they'll be lucky if they last a year." Her lips pinch in disapproval and she flutters her eyelids.

Whoa. She's a gossip, and a mean-spirited one at that.

"Those septuagenarians by the window booked two sleeping compartments. She claims he snores, but who's to say?" Dame Joanna sips her champagne and shakes her head as though the couple has a questionable ulterior motive for their accommodation choices.

She seems eager to share her knowledge, so I stick close and play to her ego. "Who's the lady with the bottle-blonde coiffe?"

The railway owner nods conspiratorially. "Margo Powell. Long before your time, dear. She was a big deal news anchor. Hardly worth a second look these days, but she's clinging heroically to the past."

Ouch! Remind me to stay on this busybody's good side.

"Steer clear of Mr. Usher. He's a washed-up base-ball player with a penchant for the ladies. He may look old enough to be your father—but don't trust him any farther than you can throw him." She finishes her drink and motions for her aging nurse to fetch another.

"Mrs. Hecht, I'm not sure if you should mix al-cohol with your medication."

Dame Joanna's eyes go wide and she lifts her chin defiantly. "Alice, you shall refer to me as 'Dame Joanna' and remember your place."

The nurse may bend a knee, but as she turns to find a waiter, I hear a distinct obscenity mumbled under her breath.

Oh, goody! The night is young, and there's al-ready plenty of drama. "Anything else I should know before I mingle?"

The condescending tongue-wagger sniffs sharply and surveys the room. "The widow by the dessert tray is as boring as watching grass grow, and the man in the dark glasses, Orson Elliot, is a leg-end-in-his-own-mind. A writer of some sort." She shakes her head as though he and his profession are beneath her.

The man she called Orson Elliot wears tinted, round wire rims and nervously smooths his expertly trimmed coffee-brown mustache. His similarly dark hair peeks out beneath his black bowler hat. Most men remove their hats when seated, but this guy looks like he could bolt any minute. He probably keeps the hat on to save himself a few seconds when he makes his exit. The corner booth and the nervous gestures indicate a typical introvert. Oddly, my super senses come up empty on additional tidbits.

Back to the high-society informant. I paste a fake smile on my stunned face and bow my head politely. "It was lovely to meet you, Dame Joanna. I'm sure we'll have another opportunity to chat." Although, between you and me, I'm seriously hoping I'm wrong about that.

She purses her lips as she appraises my wardrobe. "You and your sheriff enjoy yourselves—but not too much."

I've just met this woman and already I'd like to *Throw Mama from the Train*! I nod and offer a completely false courtesy laugh as I sashay toward the thirty-something newlyweds who can't keep their hands off each other.

"Hi. Mitzy Moon."

The petite redhead offers me a high five, which I ignore. She proceeds, unfazed. "Hi. Katie Marat." She points to her baby bump. "This is part of my character. #FalseAlarm #WhyMe. In real life, I'm a web designer. #LearningOnTheJob." Yes, she's saying the "hashtag" part out loud before everything.

Her doughy, dark-haired husband, with his

overly waxed handlebar mustache, thrusts his hand toward me. "Rob Pierre, social media influencer. Don't mind Katie. She loves it. She wouldn't have a thing to do if she wasn't complaining."

Pretending I don't know their story, I ask a polite question. "What brings you to the Scenic Railway?"

He chuckles salaciously and winks at Katie. "We're honeymooners. If the train car is rockin'—"

Thankfully, Katie interrupts. "Rob! #Over-Share!" She turns to me and smiles, but it doesn't reach her eyes. "We're just seventeen and in love! #Blessed."

These two are . . . I can't even. "I need to grab some nosh. See you 'round." Without waiting for a #Response, I hustle to the greying widow posted up next to the cookie platter.

"Good evening, I'm Mitzy Moon."

"Lulu Weathers. Nice to meet you, dear." The unassuming woman pinches her lips together and points to the center of the car. "Looks like something is about to happen."

I'll have to grill Orson Elliot, Margo Powell, the Josephs, and Mr. Usher later. A nervous-looking, pencil-necked man incessantly pushing up his glasses coughs several times to get everyone's attention. That must be the organizer. No one pays him any mind.

Oooh! At the opposite end of the shindig there's one attendee who actually looks interesting enough to make all this small talk worthwhile. I shimmy my shoulders as I pass Erick, and saunter over to the fascinating individual. "Mitzy Moon, lounge singer. And who might you be?"

The woman adjusts her regal purple and gold brocade caftan and flips her strawberry-blonde waves over her shoulder. "I am Mademoiselle Lenormand. Do you wish to know your future?"

Mad respect to this lady. She is fully in character. The ruby on her golden head wrap and glimmering opal pendant are far from costume pieces, and her French accent is exquisite. Grams has trained me well. "Gosh, that sounds like the bee's knees."

She bows her head accommodatingly and gestures to a small circular table set up in the corner of the bar car. It's covered with a purple velvet cloth, and in the center sits a glistening crystal ball. To the left, a stack of tarot cards, and to the right, a small glass disc resembling a monocle. She takes the far seat with her back against the wall, and I slip into the chair opposite.

She places the glass disc over her left eye, waves her hands dramatically over the crystal ball, and exhales. "Your husband loves you very much."

Well, there's one question answered. Her psychic skills aren't nearly as authentic as her accessories. No worries. I'll simply take this opportunity to use my powers to read *her*.

"A wonderful opportunity will present itself at your job. Possibly a promotion or raise."

Upon closer examination, her accent is definitely false. However, the lovely hair is real. The large flowing garment is meant to deceive. I sense she's younger and far more fit than the casual observer would assume.

"I see two children in your future. A smart boy and a strong, athletic girl."

She has secrets. Perhaps they are the secrets of her character, but I sense something deeper. Something she's struggling to protect.

"You shall endure a brief struggle, but you will be richly rewarded."

My smile is probably more condescending than I intend, but as a true psychic, I take offense at her song and dance. Slipping a couple twenties out of my beaded handbag, I toss them on the table and dive into my sassy flapper character. "Better luck next time, doll. My rewards are already pretty rich." Spinning on my ruby slippers, I walk back to my handsome escort with no regrets. People who play pretend with powers they can't understand don't deserve my sympathy. If I've learned anything from Silas, and I've learned a boatload, respect for the powers-that-be is paramount.

Erick holds his cigar in one hand and his barely touched champagne in the other. "So what's your future?" he jokes.

Emboldened by my intake of sparkling wine, I press against him and whisper, "How far in the future are we talking, handsome?"

My extrasensory perceptions receive a jolt of heat as he shoves his unlit cigar in his breast pocket and scoops an arm tightly around my waist. "I'd settle for tonight's forecast."

Oops. Never bet more than you can afford! He's called my bluff. I swallow loudly and lean away.

He grins wickedly. "That's what I thought."

The tiny, anxious man steps to the center of the bar car a second time and clanks a fork against his water glass. He's abandoned the subtle coughing plan. "May I have your attention? May I have your attention, please?"

The conversations and movements churn to a halt as all eyes turn toward our host.

"Welcome to Murder Mystery aboard the Scenic Railway."

A smattering of applause ripples through the gathered party.

"I see you're all in character, which is wonderful. I hope you've had time to peruse the program.

After the mixer, supper will be served in the Blue Heron restaurant car. After the dessert course, we will experience a brief power outage."

He makes exaggerated air quotes as he says power outage, and my eyes roll back in my head of their own free will.

"When the lights come back on, we will have our corpse. At that point, you'll have ample time to examine the crime scene and you may also interview the other participants throughout the weekend. The first person to correctly identify the killer will win $200 cash—"

He raises a finger and nods his head as though he's Ed McMahon awarding a million-dollar Publisher's Clearinghouse check. "And two first-class tickets, redeemable at any time within the next twelve months, on the Scenic Railway."

This news is followed with a more exuberant round of applause.

"Cheers to that!" Everyone whip pans to me and there's an awkward silence, but eventually glasses are raised and we all toast.

That's two glasses of champagne down the hatch for me. I think I can squeeze in one more before supper.

CHAPTER 5

THE AWKWARD MIXER DRAGS ON, and I hang off Erick's arm more like an accessory than an autonomous woman. The effects of the champagne on an empty stomach are definitely going straight to my head.

By the time we're swept into the restaurant car, my noggin is spinning and my tummy is holding a serious grudge.

As soon as we take our seats, Erick sets the breadbasket directly on top of my fine-china charger. "Eat something, Moon."

I nod and immediately do as I'm told. Once I get a little filler in my stomach, I'm able to admire my surroundings. The sophisticated inlaid woodwork and glossy lacquer finish complement an elegant table setting. The crystal gleams, and there are several courses of noteworthy fare. A delectable lobster bisque and a plate of venison medallions so tender I nearly faint from the joy.

When our server brings the dessert menu, my eyes light up like a child's on Christmas morning. "If I get the chocolate soufflé, will you get the bread pudding with caramel-rum sauce?"

Erick thoughtfully bites his lip and avoids openly mocking my dessert obsessions.

The waiter bows from the waist and collects our plates. "Would either of you care for coffee or tea?"

My date raises his finger, and I can't resist taking advantage of my newfound energy boost. "Do you have Irish coffee by any chance?"

The waiter nods. "Right away, Miss."

He shuffles off, and Erick leans back and crosses his arms over his chest in that tasty way that makes his biceps bulge.

"Ahem. My eyes are up here, Moon."

Grinning, I adjust my feathered headband and whisper from behind my hand, "I know, but your yummy arms are right there."

His cheeks flush, and he reaches for his ice water.

The delectable desserts disappear in record time, and as the waiters clear plates and refill coffees and waters, the lights flicker and go out.

Despite the warnings, there are several gasps and even one scream in the darkness.

When the lights come up, there is indeed a corpse with a blade in its back lying motionless on the richly woven carpet.

First on the scene is the corpse's bride. During the mixer she introduced herself as Katie Marat, a web designer. She's playing the part of a pregnant lady's maid, and her husband, Rob Pierre, was to be the detective inspector.

I have to say, I appreciate the irony in killing off the detective.

Her comical overreaction is met with a whispered grumble from her pretend-dead husband. "Simmer down, Kate. It's only a prop knife."

She presses her hand to her heart. "It looks so real! #CarriedAway."

Mademoiselle Lenormand remains firmly ensconced at her table for one. The only other participant *not* eager to examine the crime scene is the elderly Dame Joanna, who, I inform Erick, is the actual owner of the railway. It's hard to say why she chose to participate. She's clearly not interested in the game. Perhaps she wanted a first-hand account of the refurbished railway's maiden voyage. Who better to judge the true success or failure of the venture than her?

Erick and I wait until all the looky-loos have

utterly destroyed any evidentiary value, and then we take our turn. He holds his cigar in his left hand. "What d'you make of it, doll? Why don't you walk those gams over to the stiff and gimme a report?"

I had no idea he possessed such dramatic skill. Adjusting my feather boa, I slip out of my chair and approach the corpse. "I'd have to say it's revenge, boss. Gettin' stabbed in the back is a real pain."

He presses his lips together to keep from chuckling. "Tell me more, babe." While I examine the scene, Erick turns to the rest of the participants. "Looks like this dame's got real gumshoe potential."

The elderly couple chuckles, and the loud-mouthed former athlete playing a waiter nods in agreement.

Standing over the body, I take a deep breath and wait for some extrasensory secrets. The antique mood ring on my left hand sizzles with a message. I casually glance down, and see the image of a woman's hand slipping the blade from her garter as it warps across the cloudy cabochon. "If you ask me, honey, a poker like that looks like something a broad would carry."

Erick nods. "Maybe we oughta dust it for prints?"

A smattering of grumbles pass through the crowd and the organizer steps forward. "My apologies. We can't subject our guests to fingerprinting. That's not part of the game."

I lift my shoulders and blow a raspberry through my bright-red lipstick. "Looks like we'll have to beat a confession out of someone."

Erick punches his right fist into the palm of his cigar hand and nods. "Where d'you want me to start, doll?"

Nervous laughter ripples through the crowd. The anxious organizer clears his throat. "That's it for tonight, folks. The bar car is still open and we'll let you resume the game at breakfast. Have a great evening." He leans down and puts a hand on Mr. Pierre's back as he recovers the prop knife. "You can get up now, sir. According to the rules, you're not allowed to help anyone in any way, since your character is officially dead."

I'm sure Mr. Pierre will have something to say about that, but I'm too busy dragging Erick to the bar car to give a hoot.

"Did you see the way a couple of those folks reacted when we mentioned fingerprinting?"

My mobster nods his head. "I only had a good view of Kevin Usher, the waiter. What did you see?"

"I can't remember her last name, but I think her first name is Alice. She's playing nursemaid to that Dame Joanna."

Erick nods. "We better tread lightly. I have a feeling there are a few people keeping real secrets in this game."

I barely have time to nod before Bernie and Tootie Josephs accost us.

Bernie slaps his hand on Erick's shoulder. "How are you kids doin'? Tootie and I are having the time of our lives. Can I interest you in a Model T, son?"

The good-natured Erick chuckles. "You're not actually a car dealer, are you, Bernie?"

The man shakes his head. "Nah, back in the real world, I have a commercial farm in Baraboo, Wisconsin. Apricots and cherries. 'The best in the Midwest.' Anywhoo, I suppose if you were gonna buy a car, you'd want something with suicide doors and a built-in Tommy-gun turret, right, son?"

The guys share a chuckle while Tootie sets her sights on me. "Gosh, that is a gorgeous dress! You and your guy must do these kinds of parties all the time! You really seem to have the lingo down. You could probably teach me a few things!"

Her extra-loud, grating laughter reminds me of fingernails scraping down a chalkboard. "Oh, I'm no expert. Just having fun." No point in giving her any details. She has already moved on to grilling Erick and isn't exactly waiting for my reply. "Will you excuse me?"

Erick raises one eyebrow, and I nod my head toward the lone woman at the end of the bar. He winks and continues his friendly banter with the Josephs.

Approaching my target, I feign a casual tone. "Excuse me, I'm Mitzy. We didn't get a chance to finish our conversation during the mixer. It's Lulu, right?"

The woman takes a moment to swirl the ice in her vodka and soda before meeting my gaze. "Nice to meet you, again. It's Lulu Weathers. I was scheduled to take this trip with my son and daughter-in-law, but she broke her leg skiing."

Now I know whose spots Erick and I took. From what I read on the cast list, Mrs. Weathers is supposed to be playing a wealthy heiress. Everything about her wardrobe indicates otherwise. "I'm so sorry to hear that. I suppose once you asked your boss for time off, you had to take it."

Lulu's hand reaches for the cross hanging from a delicate chain around her neck. "My boss is a lot more understanding than most people think."

I laugh lightly. "You're a minister? What denomination?"

For the first time since I approached, she actually makes eye contact. "Why, yes. I'm a pastor at the Lutheran church in Grand Falls. How did you guess?"

Oh brother. Time to make like Sherlock and pretend it was all in the observation and not in the otherworldly assistance. "It must've been something about the way you said 'my boss.'"

She laughs and nods her understanding. "Looks like I'm more transparent than I thought. I'm definitely glad they didn't ask me to play the corpse. I would've been horrible at keeping secrets."

When she says the word "secrets," the hair on the back of my neck stands on end. Despite her warm smile and seeming openness, she's absolutely hiding something. "What made you decide to take this murder-mystery excursion?"

Her whole face lights up with amazed joy. "I won two tickets in a contest! I never win anything. My husband has passed, so I offered to buy one more ticket so my son and his wife could come along. I guess the Lord had other plans." She shrugs and touches her necklace again.

"Well, it was very nice to meet you, Mrs. Weathers."

"Oh, please call me Lulu. May I call you Mitzy?"

"Of course. Enjoy your trip, and I am so sorry about your daughter-in-law."

She nods. "Thank you."

The next item on my punch list is a glass of champagne. Before I can get the bartender's attention, the woman playing a spinster on her last train ride budges up next to me. "Hey, you're that rich kid from Pin Cherry, am I right?"

Rise above it, I tell myself. "I'm playing a lounge singer. Name's Mitzy Moon."

She waves away my response with a flourish of her garishly long fingernails. "No, I don't care about your character. I'm supposed to be a spinster or something, but that doesn't work with my personality. I was a TV anchor for three decades. I'm all about getting the story, sweetie. I recognized you as soon as I saw you. You've been in the *Pin Cherry Harbor Post* a few times. I live up in Broken Rock now, but I always check the local rags for good stories."

Her tactless questions and over-sharing make so much more sense now. "A reporter. Then I'm sure you're familiar with the Knudsen family."

Her eyes widen, and she nods fervently. "I was an on-air anchor, but I'd have to admit the kid is a magician with a still camera. Am I right?"

I nod my agreement but can't get a word in edgewise.

"The father is a riot if you need to know the history of anything and everything, but I bet that kid is going places."

"Quince is in his first year at Columbia. He's absolutely *going* to make a brilliant journalist."

She struggles to control her facial features, but I pick up on her surprise. "Do you know the family well?"

Eager to play my cards close to the vest during this game, I choose a vague answer. "It's a small town. You know how it is."

Her eyes narrow with suspicion. "Sure. Sure."

"I didn't catch your name . . ."

"Margo. Margo Powell."

"Did your character have any dealings with our victim?"

Her shoulders tense and her lips tighten. "Back to the game already, eh? My character is just taking one last train ride. Nothing exciting."

She's way too nervous, and she answered too quickly. I'm making a mental note of that. "Well, it was nice to get to know you, Margo. Enjoy the game."

When I turn to search for Erick, I find newlywed Katie Marat hanging on his shoulder and his every word.

Not on my watch, doll! She's old enough to be his—well, she's definitely older. Time to shut this cradle robber down.

CHAPTER 6

SNAGGING TWO GLASSES of bubbly from a passing tray, I wiggle my waddle over to Erick and step too close for comfort. "Here's that champagne you asked for. Anything else I can get you?" I bite my lower lip and wink lasciviously.

Katie's fake baby bump has slipped, and it looks like she's smuggling a puppy under her dress—and it's about to escape. She reluctantly slithers off his arm and steps back.

Good. I wasn't really interested in giving anyone a black eye, my first night on the train.

Erick tilts his head in silent protest, but takes the champagne he didn't request. "Mitzy, have you met Katie?"

I slip in close to him and twirl my long strand of

pearls back and forth. "Oh, yeah. Web designer. Mid-thirties. Just married. Wife of the deceased."

At the word deceased, Katie gasps and presses a hand to her chest. "Don't say it like that! It gives me the chills. #ItsOnlyPretend."

Staying in flapper-land, I push my advantage. "I'm wondering if this whole squeamish thing is an act, Katie? Maybe you killed your husband for some insurance money. It's been done before." I take a gulp of champagne and arch one eyebrow.

My courteous boyfriend slips an arm around my waist and secretly pokes me in the side. "Mitzy's just teasing, Katie. You know it's only a game. Don't look so worried."

I refuse to let the interloper off so easily. "Hold on. She seems pretty nervous. Must be hiding something. Maybe there's more to this baby bump—"

She swallows loudly and adjusts her maid's apron. "I better go check on Rob. He's not good—in —with people." She shuffles off before either of us can protest.

"You really like to push buttons, don't you, Moon?"

"Hey, we're supposed to be solving a murder, not #Socializing. Plus, weren't you the one who once told me everyone's a suspect until they're not?"

He chuckles and kisses me sweetly. "I'm not

sure how you're still standing, young lady. By my count, that's your fourth glass of champagne, not to mention the spiked after-dinner coffee."

I step back and place one hand on my beaded hip. "Are you my chaperone now?" Before he can spoil my fun, I put the crystal coupe to my lips and drain it dry.

He takes a deep breath and hooks his arm through my elbow. "I think it's time for Cinderella to get back in her carriage."

The effects of the alcohol are definitely coursing through my veins. "Who does that make you, my Prince Charming or my fairy godmama?"

He shakes his head and keeps me upright as we pass between the train cars and weave our way back to our compartment. Even the intermittent blasts of damp lake air can't sober up this festive flapper.

During supper, the porter paid our room a visit and made up both of the sleeping berths.

Erick closes the door and assesses the situation. "I'd ask if you want to be on the top or bottom, but I say we keep you on the bottom for your own safety."

I know he's talking about the sleeping arrangements, but it still gives me the tingles. "You are the sweeeeetest man. You know that, right? You know you're the sweeeeetest man."

He smiles patiently. "I'm going to help you out

of this dress. Don't worry, I'm not getting any ideas. But I assume your grandmother would be furious if you slept in it."

Giggling, I gaze up into his adorable blue eyes. "You know my grandma? Did you know she thinks you're yummy?" At this point, I think I "boop" his nose.

He ignores my drunken confession and gently slips the headband off my spinning head, carefully placing it on a shelf, before he turns to the task of removing my beaded gown. Gingerly lifting it over my head, he takes the time to find a hanger and places the lovely dress in the narrow closet.

Before he can decide what to do next, I tip onto the bed with a sigh.

He removes my pretty red shoes and pulls the lavender-scented linens up and over, tenderly kissing my forehead. "G'nite, wild child."

Shoot! I was hoping he'd take off my garter stockings. A girl can dream.

And with that, I drift off to the land of fantasy. You know what I mean.

When I awake, the room is dark and the motion of the train has stirred my stomach into an unwelcome swirl. Pushing myself to a seated position only serves to increase the pounding in my head.

I need water and some hot chocolate, or maybe some munchies.

As I feel around in the darkness, my fingers en-counter the bathrobe that Erick thoughtfully placed across my bed. Slipping the dressing gown over my vintage intimates, I sneak out of the compartment as quietly as possible. The cooler air in the pas-sageway offers some relief from my tumbling tummy and throbbing *cabeza*.

For a moment I can't remember which way to the bar car. Eventually a sense of direction pierces the brain fog and I stumble toward what I hope is relief. Passing through the second sleeping car, a strange muffled groan and possibly a thud come from compartment 2B. If my brain wasn't swim-ming in champagne, I might be able to pick up some extrasensory information.

Yet another notable negative side effect of drinking and sleuthing. I drag my hand along the cool windows and slowly continue toward the bar car.

Closed.

Looks like that's no joy on the cocoa. Sadly, I'll have to settle for a sip of water from the faucet back in our compartment.

As I make my unsteady way down the narrow passages, the beauty of the waxing moon glistening on the great lake takes my breath away.

I press my cheek to the cool glass and stare at

the silver-black swaths of water flowing between the sparkling white slabs of floating ice.

If the locals can be believed, it will be at least another month before all traces of winter have melted away. But this elegant moment helps me re-member why I love my new life.

In addition to building my own little family of my choice, and making wonderful friendships, the breathtaking scenery in almost-Canada deserves all the accolades it receives.

Nothing beats waking up to the soft kiss of Sheriff Too-Hot-To-Handle as my alarm clock. I could absolutely get used to this.

"Morning." I rub my hand along his stubbled jawline. "Was I impossible?"

He smooths the hair back from my forehead and trails his finger down my arm. "If you ask me, you were entirely *too* possible."

My cheeks flush, and I pull the sheet up over my face. "Yeah, drunk Mitzy can be a little skanky."

He laughs and tugs the sheet down. "I didn't mind your wild side. I just prefer sober consent from my conquests."

My throat tightens and I blink rapidly. "Un-derstood."

As he hops up from my bunk, I notice he's fully dressed and his hair is already slicked into place with his favorite pomade.

"How long have you been awake?"

"A couple hours. I had a delicious breakfast, chatted up the Josephs, and made our lunch and supper reservations."

Pushing myself to a seated position, I cradle my head with one hand. "I could definitely use a breakfast. Some home fries are just what I need to settle this disagreement between my brain and my stomach."

He nods. "I'll step out so you can get dressed, and meet you in the restaurant car in fifteen minutes."

I start to nod my head, but immediately think better of it. "Normally I'd say I could do it in five, but I think I'll be operating at half speed. Let's say ten minutes."

"10-4." His chuckling fades outside the door, as he moves down the passage.

Splashing some cold water on my face in the washstand cupboard, I survey the damage in the small mirror above the marble basin.

Not as terrible as it could be. My eye makeup is barely smeared, and my hair is practically presentable.

Taking a cue from Erick, I slip into civilian attire. I'm sure there will be time to change into costumes before lunch. This morning I need comfort and coffee. Skinny jeans, a T-shirt that says "I Do What I Want" with a cat knocking a coffee cup off the counter, a hoodie, and my high-tops. All set.

I step out of my compartment and head toward breakfast.

Erick gives me a little wave when I enter the car, and I slip onto the seat, eager to get my hands on a steaming cup of coffee.

"I ordered you scrambled eggs with ham, because they didn't have chorizo, and a side of home fries. They do have Tabasco sauce, so you can spice up that pork any way you like."

"Thank you. And thanks for taking care of me last night. I get a little nervous in a big crowd and probably overcompensate with alcohol."

He nods and lifts his coffee cup, kindly avoiding any additional commentary.

Reaching across the table, I steal a triangle of his toast while I wait for my meal. The service is nowhere near as fast as the diner back in Pin Cherry. I'll be sure to let Odell know how much he was missed.

Most of the suspects from last night's mixer are present. In fact, the only people absent are Dame Joanna and her nurse.

My breakfast finally arrives. I shove a forkful of

home fries down my gullet as I ponder the where-abouts of the snotty gossip.

No sooner has the thought tumbled through my slushy mind than all heads snap toward a bloodcur-dling scream.

Erick is up in a flash. "Wait here."

Normally I would ignore his instruction and instantly follow, but the food is delicious, and I haven't had nearly enough coffee to deal with what-ever is happening.

It only takes a few moments for the tragic news to travel through the passenger-to-passenger grapevine and reach my ears.

Dame Joanna is dead. For reals. This is not part of the game. Everyone suspects foul play.

Well, now I have to see.

I guzzle the rest of my coffee and wipe my mouth.

Following the commotion, I easily locate the nexus of the disaster.

Erick is blocking the doorway and keeping all the curious bystanders at bay. When he catches sight of me, a wave of relief washes over him. "Get the conductor. I have to preserve the crime scene."

It smells like someone dumped out an entire bottle of hideous perfume in that compartment. Was she overcome by bad cologne? No time to ask. I nod once and head for help.

A waiter in the restaurant car picks up a radio and alerts the conductor to the emergency.

He arrives in minutes with a doctor, who happened to be a passenger on the train, and another man who must be train security.

"This way." I lead them to the chaos outside 2B.

2B? Why does that sound so familiar? Oh, right! I heard a strange sound in there last night. I have no idea what time that was, but I'll mention it to Erick.

The conductor brusquely disburses the crowd, and the doctor enters the room, while the security guard attempts to send Erick away.

My handsome lawman isn't having it. "Listen, I'm Sheriff Harper of Birch County, and I'm not going anywhere until we determine whether this woman died of natural causes or was murdered."

The conductor gasps. "Murdered? I hardly think she was murdered, sir. There's no blood."

I quickly place a hand over my mouth to hide my smirk. I can think of at least ten ways to kill someone without leaving a drop of blood. How sheltered a life has this guy lived?

The doctor hesitates next to the body. "I'm not a medical examiner. I'm a pediatrician."

Erick exhales in frustration. "I'm going to need two sets of latex gloves and at least a dozen plastic storage bags. Oh, and a permanent marker."

The conductor stands stock-still.

Sheriff Harper leans toward the train manager. "I'm going to need those items right away."

The man finally snaps out of whatever trance he had fallen into and hurries off to fill the request.

The Scenic Railway security guard attempts to assert his authority. "We're currently in Canada, Sheriff. You don't have any jurisdiction here."

Erick widens his stance and looks down at the far shorter man. "According to the itinerary, this train doesn't stop until Sault Ste. Marie. That's in the United States. And I plan on solving this case, arresting the murderer, and handing this body over for a proper postmortem when we get there. If you get in my way, I'll add your arrest for obstruction of justice to that list."

My spine straightens and I swallow hard even though I'm not the one getting the warning. Erick's words have a similar effect on the puffed-up security guard.

He steps back and offers a solution. "I'll secure this car and make sure the scene isn't tampered with."

Erick nods. "Thank you. It would actually be extremely helpful if you could get statements from the occupants on either side of Dame Joanna Hecht's compartment. I'm especially interested to hear what her nurse, who discovered the body, has to say."

The security guard's ego accepts the task with gusto. "10-4, Sheriff."

He trundles off to collect his witness statements, and I pull the neckline of my T-shirt up over my mouth to lessen the cloying scent of cologne. "I thought maybe I was going to have to lock him in the baggage compartment."

The sheriff scoffs and shakes his head. "You give a guy a security guard title, and he thinks he's Sam Spade."

A brief burst of uncontrolled laughter escapes before I get a handle on myself. "I'll try to remember that while I'm amateur sleuthing all over your crime scene. Hey, how is this overly sweet odor not making you sick?"

His full lips smile, but his eyes scan the small compartment with worry. "I must have been too distracted when I first ran in, and now I'm used to it."

Continuing to filter the air through my shirt, I shake my head. "Maybe your nose is broken."

He shrugs. "Here's what I see. There's no sign of a struggle." He glances at the door. "No sign of forced entry. Maybe she did die of natural causes."

My psychic senses flutter with disagreement. "I heard a strange sound coming from this compartment last night."

He shifts his weight and tilts his head. "When was this?"

"I can't be sure. I didn't check the time. I slipped out of the compartment to see if I could get some snacks in the bar car, but it was closed. The moon was almost directly overhead and it was shining across the lake in a really magical way. But that's beside the point."

He whips out his phone. "No service! Let me see . . . the full moon is in two days. If moonrise was at 1900 hours last night, it would've been directly overhead at 0300 . . . So it was probably around 0200 when you heard the noise."

"Impressive. I had no idea you were a walking ephemeris."

Leaning back and shaking his head, he asks, "A what?"

"Oh, it's an astrologist thing I picked up in Sedona. It's nothing. What I meant was your star math was uncanny."

His eyes drift off to that place where I can't follow. "It's funny the things that become important when you're hunkered down in the desert tracking enemy troop movements. Anyway, I'll be able to confirm that calculation if I can ever get a signal." He slips his phone back into his pocket. "What sort of noise did you hear?"

I attempt to replicate the sound, and he nods. "We'll make a note of it."

Taking a step closer to the body, I feel a strange disturbance in the victim's lingering aura. "I'm pretty sure she was murdered. Look at her coloring. She has an awfully healthy appearance, for a natural death."

He glances at the unblemished body and shakes his head. "One of your hunches?"

"Yep."

CHAPTER 7

WHEN THE CONDUCTOR returns with the items Erick requested, I feel like a third wheel.

"Hey, I'm going to shove off, all right?"

He pauses his CSI duties and glances up with a serious clenching of his jaw. "Yeah, um, can you trail that rent-a-cop? I need someone to make sure he's asking the right questions."

"Me?" I scrunch up my face and shake my head. "He's not gonna let me tag along while he interviews potential suspects."

Erick tugs at the wrist of one of his latex gloves and grins. "I have complete faith in your ability to weasel your way in."

"Rude." I giggle and shrug. "If he gives me any trouble, I'm gonna drop your name."

He nods. "Of course you will."

It doesn't take long to locate the security guard. He's corralled all the first-class passengers in the Blue Heron restaurant car. And is literally questioning them as a *group*.

Smiling at the crowd, I ask, "Will you excuse us for a second." I slip my arm through his elbow and whisper for his ears only, "I know you're trying to make this as easy as possible for the passengers, but I'm sure you realize that it will give the murderer an advantage if he hears the other folks' stories. Certainly, you'd prefer to question them individually so you have a better opportunity to spot the lies. And since there aren't any empty compartments, I'm happy to donate mine to the cause. Seems like the perfect place to conduct the rest of your interviews."

During my surreptitious speech, I feel his energy shifting back and forth between resistance and compliance. Hopefully, I employed enough flattery to help him land on the side of agreement.

He nods as though he's had a brilliant idea. "You stay here and make sure they're not conspiring, and I'll take them back to your compartment one by one."

"That's a great strategy. Do you need my key?"

"The conductor and I have master passkeys."

Well, there's a tidbit I'll be sharing with Erick. "Got it. Who would you like to start with?"

"Miss Dondorf, follow me." His posture is stiff and his voice carries more authority than he possesses.

Alice Dondorf, the deceased's nurse, slowly gets to her feet and follows the officer.

There will be plenty of time for me to double-check Alice's story. For now, I'll work my way through the balance of the suspects while they're at my disposal.

The Josephs strike me as the least likely suspects, and there's room at their table.

"Good morning. What a strange way to start the day." I drop into a chair and exhale dramatically.

Tootie and Bernie eagerly spill their guts. "We were up with the sun. Didn't hear a peep in our car." Bernie nods and Tootie takes the baton. "We're in 1 and 2A. I think that TV woman is next to us. She's as quiet as a mouse. In her compartment, that is." The elderly woman winks at me, and we chuckle.

Oooh. Sic burn. This Tootie is a pistol. My clearer head, at last, confirms my suspicions. These two are as innocent as they come. "You two stick together today. Until we figure out exactly what's going on, I think we all need a locomotive buddy."

The agriculture mogul and his wife exchange smiles and clasp hands across the table.

My next target is the newlyweds. I didn't like

the look of them from the moment I laid eyes on them.

"Good morning. Did you two sleep well?"

Katie offers me a face that's all #MeanMug with a little side-eye, while Rob leans toward me with uncomfortable eagerness, pushing a cloud of cheap cologne my way.

"Where's that sexy dress you were wearing last night?"

Ew. For supposed newlyweds, they sure have a lot of interest in other people. "Did you two return directly to your compartment after the mixer?"

Katie inhales sharply. "You don't think Dame Joanna was murdered?"

I can't begin to tell you the hashtags running through my mind. Somewhere in the back of my head, I hear Grams' voice reminding me about getting more flies with honey. "Oh, heavens no. I thought I heard something around 2:00 a.m., and I'm curious if anyone else heard the same thing."

The bride bites her lip and looks away, but Rob quickly offers up his alibi. "Around two o'clock in the morning . . . I'd have to say Katie and I were pretty busy making noise of our own in our compartment." He flashes his eyebrows suggestively.

#GagMeWithASpoon. Rest assured, people who have to talk about it this much—aren't getting any. I don't think these two had anything to do with the murder, but, if they did, this gross cover story would be a great way to throw us off the scent. "Well, I guess I'll check with some of the other passengers." I can't get away from him fast enough!

Margo Powell is next on my list, and I'm not looking forward to it. "Hey, Margo, how did you sleep?"

"I know what you're up to." She places her right hand on her heart. "I swear, I had nothing to do with the murder. And I'm talking about this morning's slaying, not the pretend nonsense from last night."

"What makes you think it's a murder?"

"Come on, Mitzy. I was a beat reporter before I was on-air. You and I both know natural causes never lead to interrogations. But if it makes you happy, I barely slept at all. I've had terrible insomnia since I quit the business, and they closed the bar a tad too early for my liking."

"Did you hear any strange noises?"

"I had on my noise-canceling headphones. I was listening to an autobiography of Abraham Lincoln on audiobook. Sorry I can't be of more help, but I know less than nothing about what happened last night."

The hairs on the back of my neck tingle, and I'm pretty sure Margo's story is as false as her eyelashes. "If you think of anything, let me know, all right?"

She crosses her arms and nods. "Sure thing."

If ever there was a more cagey witness.

Who's next? Kevin Usher. The man who plays the role of a waiter in our game, but claims to be a former major league baseball player, happens to be nearest. However, I pretend to be distracted and make my way toward the minister in our midst instead. "How are you holding up, Lulu?"

She reaches out and touches my arm. "I'm so sorry to hear about Dame Joanna. She seemed like a nice woman. It's all so sad."

Nice woman? I only heard the lady gossiping and barking instructions to her nurse, and I would hardly qualify them as kind. "Did you know the deceased?"

Lulu looks away. "No, I didn't know anyone on the train. That's why I was so hesitant to travel alone. And now with this—"

"Don't worry, we'll get to the bottom of it."

Rather than relief, my statement causes the pastor to clench her jaw and fidget in her chair.

"Mrs. Weathers, is there something you'd like to tell me?"

"I thought I heard something last night. I should've checked. I feel responsible."

That would explain the shift in her energy. "I

thought I heard something too. No one's to blame for this, except the person responsible. You and I can't take that on."

She sniffles a bit and nods. "I don't know if the woman who passed was religious, but if there's anything I can do—"

"I'll be sure to let you know. Thank you."

Just as I'm about to run out of suspects, Alice returns and Bernie Josephs is asked to accompany the officer.

Tootie stands and announces defiantly, "Well, I'm comin' with him."

"I'm interviewing the passengers one at a time." The guard's voice wavers.

"If Tootie isn't comin' with me, I ain't going nowhere. There could be a murderer loose on this train! I'm not leaving my wife alone."

Several of the passengers gasp.

I step forward and gesture for everyone to simmer down. "Joanna Hecht's cause of death hasn't been determined. Let's not jump to conclusions." Turning to the security guy, I shrug. "I'm sure you can interview Bernie and his wife together."

The officer clears his throat and nods indifferently. "Mr. and Mrs. Josephs, follow me."

Time for me to move in on Alice. "Mrs. Dondorf, had you been working for Dame Joanna long?"

The mousy woman crosses her arms and narrows her gaze. "I was only playing a nurse for the game, so we can dispense with that nonsense. Joanna was my sister and her title was 'honorary.' She loved to lord it over people and force all her employees to call her 'Dame,' but that is just her way—was her way."

Noted. I'm afraid I will also have to take note of the fact that this woman isn't very broken up over her sister's death. "I'm so sorry for your loss, Alice. Were you and your sister close?"

She scrunches up her face in what can best be described as disgust. "We were sisters. Sisters are always close."

That statement carries about as much authenticity as a fake Gucci purse being sold out of the trunk of a car in Manhattan. "You weren't staying in compartment 2B, were you?"

"I had my own room. I was in 3B."

"But why weren't you in 1B? I thought there was a door between one and two. Wouldn't that have been more convenient for you and your sister?"

"I didn't make the reservations. I wouldn't know. Joanna's assistant made all the arrangements."

"All right. But you still might've heard something—around 2:00 a.m.?"

"I'm sorry to say, I'm a very sound sleeper." She stands and glares at me. "I don't believe you're officially connected to this investigation. I need some tea." And with that, she turns on her sensible shoes and marches toward a waiter.

As I'm bolstering my courage to chat up the loudmouthed and unpredictable Kevin Usher, all heads turn toward the dramatic entrance of Mlle. Lenormand.

Despite the hour, she is already in full wardrobe for her character. She brushes past the gathered crowd without a word and heads straight to the table in the corner. She snaps her fingers toward a server, and the young girl rushes to the woman's side. A few commands are mumbled, and the server removes everything from the table.

Mlle. Lenormand opens her carpetbag and sets up her divination table exactly as it was last evening in the bar car.

Wait . . . I think the tarot cards were on the left. Sadly, last night is all a tad hazy. Either way, it's time for me to put this dodgy diviner in her place. I approach the table and drop into the chair nearest me as she takes her place.

"Do you wish to know your future?" The soft French accent remains.

"I think we covered that last night. I'd prefer to know your past."

She attempts to school her smooth, creaseless face with an air of nonchalance. However, my extrasensory perceptions receive an unexpected wallop.

A jolt of panic hits the cleverly disguised young woman. If not for my true psychic powers, I would never have noticed. Her youthful face remains stoic. Underneath it all, for a moment, she seems not to remember me. How odd.

"I'm not sure what you mean, Miss."

"Mitzy Moon. We met last night. Do your powers prevent you from remembering past events?"

A flash of anger lights up her grey-green eyes and her right hand grips the tarot deck tightly. "I have studied the art of divination for decades. I don't appreciate your mockery. I performed several readings last night. When the muse of prophecy speaks through me, I am merely a vessel. I have no memory of her prognostications."

If she thinks I'm going to apologize, she's sadly mistaken. "Which compartment are you staying in?"

Her chapped pink lips press into a firm line.

"You don't have to answer, but I'm working with the sheriff and the train's security officer to discover the cause of Dame Joanna's death. If you choose not to cooperate, that's fine. I can easily get the information from the passenger manifest. But, you know, lack of cooperation does look a little sketchy. Would you like to answer my questions or would you like me to add your name to the top of the suspect list?" I don't like her attitude, and my empty threats about a suspect list won't hold any water if she pushes me, but I'm hoping to frighten her into cooperating.

"I'm a very private person, Miss Moon. I'll answer what I can."

"Thank you. Which compartment are you assigned for this excursion?"

"I am staying in 1B."

"Did you hear any disturbance in the adjoining compartment?"

"Certainly not. I have to sleep with earplugs. I'm very sensitive to external energetic disturbance when I slumber—because of my gifts."

That sounds like a load of hogwash. "Was the door between your compartment and Dame Joanna's secured last night?"

"I must admit, I have no idea. It was secured when I checked in. It would never have occurred to me to test it again later."

"Does anyone else have access to your room?"

Her eyes dart away from me and she fidgets in her chair. "Well, certainly the porter has access. And the conductor has a passkey."

Interesting that she knows about the conductor's passkey. "Are you a frequent train traveler, Mlle. Lenormand?" Over the course of our questioning, her French accent has become thinner and thinner.

"This is my first trip. And after all of these inconveniences, I'm certain I will not be taking another."

"Thank you for your cooperation. One last question. How old are you?"

Her eyes widen, and she crosses her arms tightly over her chest. "One should never ask a lady's age!"

Accent . . . vanished.

I shrug indifferently and walk away from the table. Lucky for me, my mentor Silas Willoughby taught me how to snatch an answer from someone's mind even if they choose not to speak it aloud. I'm generally sixty-ish percent successful. When I asked her age, she immediately thought thirty-four. Her wardrobe and the way she carries herself in costume make her seem at least twenty years older. Why the ruse? She could've easily played a thirty-four-year-old fortuneteller for the mystery game.

A quick scan of the compartment reveals Orson Elliot is missing. It didn't occur to me when I surveyed the room earlier. I'll have to check his compartment.

All right. I've put off talking to Mr. Usher as long as possible. Taking a deep breath, I walk toward my final target in the Blue Heron. "Hi, Mr. Usher. Did you know the deceased?"

He shrugs. "I knew *of* her. I probably read an article or whatever. Something about some moneyed broad buying a railroad."

Could that answer possibly be more fabricated? "Are you acquainted with any of the other first-class passengers?"

He avoids making eye contact and takes two sips of his coffee before he finds his words. "I met everyone at that mixer."

Once again, less true words were never spoken. "Did Mlle. Lenormand read your future?"

His jaw clenches and his pupils dilate for a split second. "Nah. I don't believe in that airy-fairy nonsense. No chick with a crystal ball is gonna tell me anything I don't already know. Life sucks and then you die."

"That's harsh. Why are you participating in a murder-mystery game if you have such a sour outlook on life?"

He puffs up his chest and frowns. "Haven't you heard? I'm as close to a celebrity as they could book for this thing. I played big-league ball about ten years ago."

"Oh, really? For which team?"

"Like it matters. I was holding down second base when a runner made an illegal slide and blasted me into left field. Tore up my ACL, MCL, and patellar tendon . . . ended my career right there. Most promising rookie, taken out in game two!"

For something that happened over a decade ago, this guy is still bubbling over with bitterness. "Sorry to hear it. Which compartment are you staying in?"

His whole energy changes from anger to aggression. "4A. Why? You wanna pay me a visit? Happy to slip you a key."

"Absolutely not. I'm working with law enforcement to determine the cause of death in the Dame Joanna case. I'm simply trying to get an idea where everyone was last night around 2:00 a.m."

He swallows hard and his pupils once again flash wide. "You should probably mind your own business."

"Copy that."

Time to check in with Erick and let him know what I've discovered about our seriously suspicious passenger list. Back in compartment 2B, Erick has completed collecting evidence and covered the body with a clean sheet.

I step to the door between compartments one and two to check the lock. It's definitely secured from this side. It would've been pretty difficult, actually impossible, for the murderer to pass into compartment 1B and lock this door behind. The mechanism can only be accessed from inside compartment 2B. So much for that theory.

"Do I need to dust that lock for prints?" Erick stands and pauses before removing his gloves.

"I don't think so. It was a theory that appears to be impossible."

"Humor me." He lifts his chin and waits.

"I was thinking that maybe the murderer accessed this compartment from 1B. But the door was locked from this side, and it looks like it would be impossible to open from the other side. Which means it would be impossible to lock it behind you, if you left this way."

"So that means the killer had a master passkey?"

"You know about the master keys?"

He smiles warmly and gestures to his sidekick. "To be honest, I didn't have any idea till the conductor here showed up with his. But if he and the security guard are the only ones with master keys, then we're back to square one."

"Not exactly. The porters must have master keys too. Maybe we need to question them and find out if anyone's missing their key."

The conductor lifts his hand. "The porters do have master keys."

Erick lets out a low whistle. "See? You're a natural."

I blush and grin. "I think it's more of us making a good team."

He nods. "Agreed. I'm going to secure this compartment and make sure no one has access until we get to Sault Ste. Marie. Do you have any more hunches before we leave?"

My moody mood ring and my extrasensory perceptions offer no additional tidbits. Maybe someday I'll feel confident enough to tell Erick the full story behind my hunches, but today is not that day. "Not really. Let's round up those porters and see if any of them have information that's hunch-friendly."

We step out of the compartment, and the conductor secures the door.

Erick removes his gloves and drops them into an evidence bag as he turns to the conductor. "I need you to make sure absolutely no one goes in or out of this compartment. No cleaning personnel, no porters, no other passengers."

"Yes, sir." The conductor nods firmly.

As I head toward the restaurant car, Erick offers one last instruction. "That goes for the railroad security, too. I mean no disrespect, but he has no idea of proper crime-scene etiquette. We need to preserve what remains of the evidence for the authorities."

The conductor nods and nibbles on the edge of his mustache. "We'll have to get his passkey."

Quietly chuckling, I hide my amusement. I like how the conductor used the term "we" when referencing retrieving the key. Clearly he appreciates the presence of an authentic lawman backing him up.

Placing my hand on Erick's arm, I offer some news. "FYI, that security officer is currently questioning passengers in our compartment. In case you were wondering where he might be."

He grins and shakes his head.

While he and the conductor stride off in the opposite direction, I move toward a fresh cup of liquid alert and some pastries. I'll need an energy boost if I'm going to solve this case by supper.

CHAPTER 8

THE RESTAURANT CAR has cleared out, and it looks like the passengers have either returned to their compartments, or are perhaps taking in the sights in the viewing car at the end of the train. The itinerary promises several picture-worthy vistas today.

"What can I get you, miss?"

"I'll take a coffee and some kind of pastry. What do you have?"

"Do you take cream or sugar?"

"Yes, cream only." I'm about to repeat my request for flaky sustenance, when the server begins listing off my options.

"We are currently offering a selection of artisanal doughnuts, chocolate croissants, breakfast brioche, cinnamon coffee cake, or chocolate chip muffins. What may I get you?"

Obviously, I'd like to try a little bit of every-thing. But I choose to err on the side of manners. "I'll have a chocolate croissant, please."

The server makes a shallow bow. "As you wish, miss."

Seated on the lake side of the train car, I am once again struck by the beauty of the massive body of water. Today's bright-blue sky with wisps of cirrus clouds offers a false sense of warmth. The mini-bergs floating in the vast watery expanse re-veal the true temperature.

The sudden and repetitive pinging of my cell phone interrupts the peaceful view.

Holy cat-astrophe! I have seven missed calls from Pyewacket.

Now, I realize how insane that sounds, but he's a fiendishly smart feline. He learned how to use the videoconferencing system when I took my trip to Arizona, and he's clearly been abusing it since I left Pin Cherry yesterday.

Checking my phone, I have three bars of ser-vice. I better place this call fast. Who knows when we'll slip out of range of whatever tower is currently blessing us with a signal.

Tapping the "Headquarters" entry, I wait. The screen springs to life and I turn the volume down as low as possible. If someone sees me looking at a video of a cat, no big deal. If someone notices I'm replying to "Reows" . . . I don't need that drama.

"Hey, Pye. What's going on?"

He leaps down from the desk and disappears.

Keeping my voice low, I hiss-whisper into the phone. "Where did you go? You called me like eight times, you crazy cat. What d'you want?"

In the background, Grams' faint voice calls from the closet. "Mitzy? Mitzy, is that you? Oh, thank goodness. Mr. Cuddlekins has been acting insane! He's running all over the apartment, chasing invisible somethings. Twiggy came up and announced he's not eating his Fruity Puffs, and every time he uses that Phoom thingy, he snarls like a crazy cat when you don't answer."

"Well, now I've called him and he disappeared!" An exasperated sigh leaks out. "Sorry. Let me try that one more time. Hi, Grams!" The sound of her voice never fails to warm my heart. I've always been able to hear her, as clear as if she were alive and standing next to me. No one else can pick up on her supernatural speech—with the possible exception of our fiendish feline.

The server returns with my coffee and croissant. "Would you like me to pour the cream, miss?"

Tipping the screen away from his view, I smile and shake my head. "I've got it. Thank you."

He shuffles away, while I take a glorious whiff

of buttery pastry and return to my call. "The reception is terrible on the train. This is the first time I've had any service today. If Pye doesn't get back here soon with whatever his urgent business is, he'll miss the chance. I could lose the call at any moment."

Before Grams can reply, the tufted ears and fierce whiskers of my fur baby appear on-screen.

"You're too close to the camera, Pyewacket. I can't see what you have in your mouth. Back up a little."

He takes two steps backward, and the item clenched between his pointy teeth swims into focus.

"A pirate flag? I don't know what it means, and I haven't seen any pirates on the train, but I'll log it into evidence."

He drops the flag. "RE-OW!" Game on!

The image glitches twice before the call drops completely.

It's good to know everyone's all right back at the bookshop. Shoot! I was so distracted by Pye's antics that I forgot to tell Grams about the actual murder on my murder-mystery adventure. I have no idea what a pirate flag has to do with my current case, but I've learned never to underestimate the clues dropped by my feline friend.

Returning the phone to my pocket, I pour a little cream in my coffee and watch it swirl into the dark brown depths of my steaming china cup. The croissant is light and flaky and satisfying. By the time I finish my second cup of java, Erick finds his way to the restaurant car.

"Is this seat taken?"

I shake my head at his foolish pickup line. "Sit down. Sit down. I have so much to tell you."

He gestures to the server and orders a glass of water and a chocolate chip muffin. "What's the scoop, Moon?"

"In my opinion, the Josephs are in the clear."

He nods. "That checks out. Who tops your list?"

"Kevin Usher was definitely hiding something. Margo Powell is far too practiced at deception, and Mlle. Lenormand kept her answers overly vague. Oh, Orson Elliot was never questioned. I meant to knock on his compartment, but—"

"You had a croissant emergency?" He takes a large bite of his muffin and grins. "What about the preacher?"

"Lulu? I don't know. She seemed more concerned about death in general, than anything else. I think she's just lonely and quiet."

He nods and then shakes his head, as though he's disagreeing with himself. "We'll see. Do you want to hear about the porters?"

Eagerly nodding, I lean forward.

"You were right. One of the porters was missing his key."

"I knew it. Whoever has the key is our killer!"

Reaching across the table, he puts his hand on my arm. "Easy, Moon. Let's try to be a little discreet."

I look over my shoulder and meet the stares of several occupants of the restaurant car. Apparently, quite a few folks slipped back into the dining car while I was shoving pastry into my mouth with wild abandon. "Copy that."

He takes a swig of his water. "Unfortunately, some passenger from coach class found the key on the floor of the water closet. He turned it in to the bartender, and the bartender didn't get a name. Also claims he's not good with faces."

"Classic." I finish my coffee and sigh. "You want me to take pictures of all the first-class passengers and show them to the bartender?"

Erick shakes his head and scowls. "That's the problem. All the staff have pictures of the first-class passengers. They were instructed to give excellent service to the people on that photo roster. The bartender said the man who turned in the key wasn't on the roster."

I lean back in my chair and my shoulders fall. "So it could be any one of a couple hundred random passengers in the coach cars."

Erick shrugs. "Exactly."

Waving my hand across the table, I'm impatient to share my news. "Let's put a pin in that. It's possible there's no connection. And, while we're on the topic of things that seem to have no connection, Pyewacket held a miniature pirate flag up in front of the camera when I called him earlier."

He pulls out his phone. "No service, again! So you're telling me I missed the window?"

Leaning forward, I put my hand on his phone and push it down to the table. "The only person you need to call is right here. Why are you so concerned about getting service? I thought you said the engineer would radio ahead about the possible murder."

He blushes and looks down. "I promised my mom."

Chuckling, I press back against my chair. "If I didn't know you better, Harper, I'd be worried. Is she still in the cast?" I want to say "the cast that ruined our Valentine's plans," but there were way too many things that took a swipe at that getaway. I'm honestly shocked we managed to get on this train. But, it seems like rather than escaping crime, the murder followed us on board.

He walks his fingers across the table and turns up his palm. "Where did you go?"

Slipping my hand in his, I give it a squeeze. "Not important. What did I miss?"

"My mom's wrist is healing up great. She's out of the permanent cast and the doctor said she'll only need the brace for one more week. One of the neighbors is looking in on her, but I do worry."

"Understandably."

Warm silence hangs between us, and his thumb rubs tenderly across my fingers. "Wait, did you say a 'pirate flag'?"

Choking briefly on my response, I nod. "Yeah. I couldn't make heads or tails of it either."

Erick accidentally spits a little water and grabs his napkin to cover his mouth.

"What? What did I say?"

After he catches his breath, his cheeks redden. "It was just the way you said 'heads or tails.' Because you were talking about a cat . . . Forget it, it was super geeky."

Tilting my head and pretending not to understand, I poke a little more fun. "I guess it's one of those things where you had to be there."

His jaw clenches momentarily before a lightbulb sparks in his big blue eyes. "Pirates. I get it!"

Not sure if I've heard him correctly, I have to ask, "Can you fill me in?"

He nods eagerly. "Pirates. Skull and crossbones!"

"Now who's drawing unnecessary attention?"

He chuckles and leans toward me. "The symbol

on a pirate flag is the skull and crossbones. That's also the symbol for poison. You suspected murder. I think Pyewacket is pointing us in the direction of poisoning."

Smiling proudly, I offer some feline praise. "It's good to know my cat is an equal opportunity helper. Maybe that clue was meant for your eyes only."

"I promised him I'd assist you in his absence." Erick suddenly hops out of his chair. "Come on. We need to take a closer look at that body. You find us two new sets of gloves, and I'll get the conductor."

We meet up at compartment 2B and I pass him a fresh pair of gloves. "What are we looking for, Sheriff?"

"Not sure. I'm not a pathologist."

And I'm not super eager to touch a dead body. So, I stand back and look over Erick's shoulder as he examines the corpse. The word "abdomen" flashes into my consciousness. "Check her stomach."

He pauses and tilts his head to look up at me. "Hunch?"

"Yep."

He carefully lifts the thick sweater to reveal numerous puncture marks. "Looks like she might've been a diabetic."

Crossing my arms, I click my tongue. "What better way to poison someone than slip it into their usual meds."

Erick carefully pulls Dame Joanna's sweater back down and stands. "You take the left side and I'll take the right. Look for syringes, a testing kit, vials of insulin . . . Pretty much anything that might be related."

"Copy that."

His search reveals her blood-sugar testing device, individually packaged alcohol wipes, and a packet of small bandages.

My search is less successful, but that in itself offers evidence. "I can't find a single used syringe, a sharps disposal container, or an open vial of insulin. For someone who's clearly a diabetic, doesn't that strike you as odd?" I show him the small cooler bag packed with unopened vials and reusable ice packs.

He double-checks the wastepaper bin and chews the inside of his cheek. "The killer took the evidence. They probably threw it off the train."

"Maybe. There's always a chance that a search of the rail line could turn it up. I know it's unlikely—"

"Real unlikely along hundreds of miles of track." He places the items that he recovered into a clean plastic bag. "There's a slim chance that the evidence is still on the train. If the killer wanted to make sure all evidence was destroyed, he or she might've hidden it and planned to get rid of it later.

It's riskier, for now, but it would ensure that no evidence remained."

"What do you think she was poisoned with?"

Erick shakes his head. "If we had some Wi-Fi access, I'd look up common symptoms." He crouches next to the body. "You should probably look away. I'm going to see if there's any discoloration on the tongue."

"Thanks for the warning. I definitely want to avert my gaze."

He does whatever he has to do. "All clear. The tongue is swollen. I guess we won't know anything for sure until we get a toxicology report."

"Makes sense. In the meantime, I suppose we should proceed as if."

He stands and tilts his head. "As if?"

"Yeah. As if she was poisoned."

"Sounds good. A working theory is better than no theory at all."

I tap a finger to my lips. "The weird thing is, the only person who had any connection to her was the lady who played her nurse, but who's actually her sister, Alice. Why would her sister want to kill her?"

"Interesting question." Erick rubs his left thumb along his jawline. "I think we better find out."

He knocks firmly on the door of compartment 3B.

An exasperated voice replies. "No house-keeping today, thank you."

"It's not housekeeping, Ms. Dondorf. It's Sheriff Harper. We'd like to ask a few questions."

A dramatic exhale and stomping feet are the only reply. The door opens a few inches, and Alice scowls at both of us. "What is it? I'm trying to take a nap. I didn't sleep well."

Now there's a red flag. "When I spoke to you, Alice, you said you were a very sound sleeper. You claimed that was why you didn't hear anything from your sister's compartment last night. Were you lying to me then, or are you lying to us now?"

She exhales and avoids a reply. Stepping back, she opens the door, but does not invite us in.

Erick needs no invitation. He walks in and takes a seat on the bench. "Alice, are you familiar with the details of your sister's will?"

Her devil-may-care attitude vanishes, and my psychic senses pick up on intense anxiety. "She has no one but me. It's not suspicious that she would leave everything to me in her will. She lost her husband decades ago and never remarried. She was unable to have children. I'm her closest living relative."

"Did you grow impatient?"

"How dare you accuse me! I would never lay an

unkind hand on my sister. We may have had our differences, but I would certainly never kill her."

Erick nods. "What differences?"

Alice walks to the window and sinks onto the bench seat opposite him. "Her husband, God rest him, was a railroad engineer on the East Coast. This whole Scenic Railway idea was some cocka-mamie scheme of hers to finally honor his memory. I thought it was a terrible waste of money and tried to talk her out of it. She wouldn't hear of it and threatened to leave all her money to charity if I didn't support her decision."

"That sounds a little like motive."

Alice waves her arms. "Motive? She already bought the railway. She's already sunk a fortune into this doomed operation. If I was going to kill her for the money, wouldn't I have done it before all of this?" She leans back in her seat and presses a hand to her forehead. "I really must rest. I have a weak heart."

Erick nods, scoops an arm around me, and closes the door behind us. He puts a finger to his lips and walks to the end of the car. "What do you think?"

I shake my head in dismay. "Of the heart? I don't think she has a heart at all. I've never seen anyone so unaffected by the death of a close relative."

"I agree. But she made a good point. If it's about the money, it would've been more beneficial to kill her sister before hundreds of thousands were dumped into this venture."

"You're not wrong. But this murder venue offers a bigger pool of suspects."

He nods. "Keep her on the suspect list, but move her to the bottom."

"I really need some kind of murder wall, Sheriff. You might be able to keep track of all this moving and deleting and adding in your mind, but I need a visual aid."

Erick reaches his arm around me and slides the phone out of my back pocket.

A flutter of tingles flip-flops through my tummy as he hands me my phone.

"Maybe you can make some notes. You know, on the notes app."

"Rude." I don't move away.

"Let's get some lunch. Maybe inspiration will strike over the elk and truffle risotto."

I rise as high as my tiptoes will take me and kiss his pouty mouth. "Anything is possible."

CHAPTER 9

THE SCENERY OUTSIDE the train has shifted from
an expanse of choppy waves to a steep-walled
canyon. The steaming locomotive will cut through
some rough country before it meanders back toward
the shoreline. Needless to say, there's no chance of
phone reception for the next couple of hours.

The restaurant car is only half full, and, after
the morning's prying inquiries, those who are
present don't make eye contact. "Looks like I managed to win friends and influence people once
again."

Erick takes a moment to swallow and wipe his
mouth. "Get used to it, Moon. People who ask too
many questions don't get invited back. Trust me."

Until I heard him say those words, I never really thought much about Erick Harper's social life.

"You have a bunch of buddies on the broomball team. Don't you guys hang out on weekends or something?"

He presses his lips together and turns to gaze out the window. "People are always pleasant. They say the right things, extend the proper hypothetical invitations, but when you get right down to it, there's not a lot of people who actually make good on their promises."

"Why not? You're fun."

He chuckles and shakes his head. "I'm fun? I don't think I've ever heard it put quite so succinctly. To be honest, I don't go looking to fill my social calendar. I'm sure if I called one or two of the guys from the broomball team, we'd hang out once in a while. But you'd be surprised how nervous people get having a few beers with a lawman at the local bar and then getting in their car to drive home."

"Is it because of that one guy you arrested?"

Erick furrows his brow. "One guy? After I made the rookie mistake that ended in a fatal drunk-driving accident, I built the highest DUI arrest record in the history of Birch County. Did I possibly overreact? Maybe, but being responsible for someone losing their life leaves a mark on you. On your soul."

Taking back my signature move, I walk my fingers across the table and turn my palm up. He slides his hand into mine and our eyes meet. My psychic senses can't be the only reason I'm feeling such a powerful connection to this man.

"It must be hard to see the dark underbelly of humanity on a daily basis."

He squeezes my hand and shrugs. "I wouldn't state it in such dire terms. There are a lot of wonderful moments in Pin Cherry and the surrounding area. For the most part, folks are kind and human. But humans make mistakes. There have been some ugly cases, but the thing that helps me sleep at night is bringing justice to victims' families."

"I don't think I ever asked why you became a sheriff, but now I understand. Does it feel like penance?"

He inhales slowly and nods. "Maybe. Two tours in the Army and losing a lot of battle buddies definitely played a part in my choices when I came back. I don't want to live in the past, but I don't want to miss an opportunity to make my future, and other peoples', better."

As he speaks, he grips my hand tighter and tighter. The flood of emotion that flows from him into me is hard to process.

I blink my eyes rapidly in an attempt to disperse the building tears. "Better futures. That's one thing we have in common. I know our childhoods were probably very different. Your mom was there to love you, worked multiple jobs to provide for you, and gave you a stable home. My mom was taken from me when I was eleven, and the foster homes I bounced through were mostly horrible. Although, there were a couple of bright spots. I'll always be grateful for foster-mom number three. She gave me a sense of place and the courage to embrace my intelligence. But when I arrived in Pin Cherry, my whole outlook on life changed."

He leans forward and his eyes twinkle impishly. "Was that before or after you tripped and fell all over me?"

I gasp and lean back. This reminds me of *He Said, She Said*. "Me? If I remember events correctly, you tripped, and took me down with you."

His eyes grow soft and his voice is deep and throaty. "I guess I knew what I wanted the moment I laid eyes on you."

And I'm dead. I don't think I've ever had a better understanding of women's historical need to faint than right now. I could avoid facing these intense emotions and responding to his declaration simply by collapsing.

No such luck.

"Mitzy? It must be hard for you to trust people. You've never spilled the details of your years in foster care, but I've had my share of run-ins following up on bad placements. It doesn't take much to imagine what you went through."

I have no words, so I nod.

"You know you can trust me, right? I might not know everything about you, but I know enough to realize that I don't want to let go. I don't want to lose you."

His voice is thick with emotion, and the flood of clairsentient information pouring across the table is overloading my circuits. "Thanks. Um, I need some air."

Erick glances at my plate. "You didn't finish your lunch. Are you sick?"

His teasing breaks the tension, and I laugh as I slide out of my chair. "I'm a huge fan of elk. It's earthy and rich. However, I'm not sure if truffle is on my Top Ten list."

He smiles. "You get some air, and I'll see if the engineer was able to contact the authorities. The clock's ticking on this murder, Moon. We could sure use one of your hunches about now."

"Copy that."

Erick kisses my hand before he releases it, and I wink as I walk toward the caboose-turned-viewing-car at the end of the train.

All is quiet in the first-class sleeping cars, but as I brave the passage between the last sleeper and the baggage car, the train passes through a particularly narrow stretch of canyon. The noise of the chugging and whirring echoes loudly. For a moment, all other sound seems to be sucked straight out of the world. The rock walls are whizzing past and the broad railroad ties below flash by so quickly they look like matchsticks.

I stumble into the baggage car and lean against one of the luggage racks to catch my breath.

There may have been a sound of warning, but the last thing I remember is something cracking into the back of my skull.

The next thing I know, the rocking of the train awakens me, but it isn't comforting, it's claustrophobic. Something feels off. Maybe it's a dream?

Since I'm fresh out of *Inception* tops, I pinch myself. Assuming that trope holds true, the pain proves I'm awake. I blink furiously, but the blackness refuses to dissipate. Shouldn't some light seep under the door of the sleeping compartment?

My head is throbbing. Totally my fault. I should've listened to Erick and slowed my roll on the bubbly.

Hold on! I can't extend my legs. I'm not in a sleeping compartment.

Pressing my hands above, below, and to both sides offers no relief. I'm one hundred percent stuck in a large luggage trunk.

The only way to manage the crippling panic is to force my brain into the mundane task of reviewing the possible actions that brought me to my current coffin—I mean, resting place. Nope! That's worse.

Come on, little brain. Don't freak. Let's take a pleasant stroll down memory lane.

Bits and pieces of last night come floating back.

How much champagne did I have?

When I rub the back of my head, there's a golf-ball-sized lump. Looks like it wasn't the champagne!

Let's see, I couldn't sleep, and I wandered out of the sleeping compartment in the middle of the night to see if someone in the bar car would make me some hot chocolate.

Man, my head really hurts.

The bar car was closed, so I think I stumbled around to see if I could find a porter.

Did I walk into the baggage car?

I don't remember doing that. If only I could use my psychic recall to playback the events. But the blow to my head has gummed up the works, and the increasing terror over being trapped inside this musty trunk is definitely messing with my focus.

Wait! I was all right this morning. I had breakfast. And I questioned the passengers.

Oops. I clearly made at least one enemy during my snooping.

The logical thing to do is conserve my oxygen, calmly try to find a means of escape, and hope to high heaven that Erick notices I'm missing.

The winner of this inner battle between logic and hysteria is anyone's guess.

Sanity suggests more distractions.

Pulling out my "No Service" phone and doing a bit of dizzy-headed math, I estimate that I've been missing three hours. If Erick were looking for me, he certainly would've found me by now. The train's not that big.

What if the person who knocked me unconscious and shoved me into what I'm calling a steamer trunk also attacked Erick?

What if no one is coming to rescue me?

Having a cell phone with no signal is about as useful as hen poop on a pump handle. I can't remember which of my foster dad's used that saying every time I disappointed him with my lack of effort in my chores, but I think I finally understand its true meaning.

Let's say Erick isn't looking for me. What am I going to do? I'm not a helpless damsel in distress. Every problem has a solution.

If I had matches, I could start a fire. Which would most likely consume me long before help was on its way.

I can scream my lungs out, but I doubt anyone in the next train car would hear even a whisper of my efforts. Plus, I'm still mildly concerned that this trunk is airtight, and I don't want to waste what little oxygen I have on fruitless schemes.

Rocking back and forth could possibly knock the trunk from its perch. If the perch is a high place, that could end badly. However, let's be honest, I'm no waif. By the time someone managed to stuff me into this trunk, it's unlikely they had enough energy to then hoist said trunk up and over their head.

A trunk knocked into the middle of the aisle should force anyone who enters the baggage car to at least be somewhat likely to investigate.

All right, if I think about it any longer, I'll talk myself out of it.

Let's do this.

I slip my useless phone inside my T-shirt and under a bra strap to protect it from possible breakage, and I start rocking back and forth.

It's kind of working.

Thank heavens I have some meat on my bones!

After several tries, I get the right combination of momentum and geometry, and the trunk tumbles into the walkway.

Tumbles might be a slight exaggeration. It tips over. Now I'm trapped in the trunk, on my side. I'm not sure if that's an improvement to being trapped in the trunk on my rear end.

Wait!

There is a tiny improvement. When the trunk

smashed onto its side, something cracked. I can see daylight.

No time like the present. I bash my fists and forearms upward, with as much force as I can muster in this cramped space. The crack is widening.

At least I have air!

The racket I'm making with my pounding and gasping for air masks all other sounds. So when someone outside tilts the trunk upright, I scream bloody murder.

"Mitzy? Mitzy, is that you?"

I've never been so happy to hear Erick's voice in my entire life.

"It's me! Someone hit me on the back of the head and stuffed me into this trunk!"

"Cover your eyes. I have an axe."

This information brings a fresh set of screams. "It's too cramped in here! Watch where you aim that thing."

"Don't worry. I'm only working on the lock."

I close my eyes and put my hands over my face. My heart is racing, and if there is any oxygen in this thing my chest is way too frozen with fear to pull it into my lungs.

CLANG!

The sharp cracking scrape of metal against metal is terrifying. But the next few seconds are worth all the momentary panic in the world.

Erick rips open the trunk lid with one arm and scoops me out with the other. He holds me so tight I can barely breathe. Which is fine. I don't need air. I have him. The intensity of his grasp erases the last specks of dread. I knew he'd find me. I knew it.

The conductor's face must reflect the relief in Erick's, but when I look up, I see a hard edge hidden beneath Erick's solace. My clairaudience hears the warning rumble: revenge.

"I need you to inform the engineer of this development immediately. What we were considering a possible homicide can definitely be upgraded. There is a murderer on the train, and they may not stop with one victim."

The color drains from the conductor's small, round visage, but he nods and scurries away to do the sheriff's bidding.

"Did you see who attacked you?"

Shaking my head, I gulp some precious oxygen into my lungs. "No, but I think that's the only reason I'm alive."

"What do you mean? Did someone threaten you?"

"They hit me from behind. I'm pretty sure if I'd seen their face, they wouldn't have left me alive."

Erick places his large hand gently over the back

of my head and pulls me close. "That is a heckuva lump, Moon."

I nod my head against his chest and listen to the comforting thump-thump of his heart.

"Let's get you back to our compartment, and I'll find an ice pack or bag of ice. Did you lose consciousness?" He's steering me in front of him down the narrow passage, but one hand has a firm grasp around my waist, and I can sense his fierce protective energy coiled at the ready.

"Are you serious? I've been missing for like three hours! Of course I was unconscious."

An indistinct grumble is his only response.

"Sorry. I didn't mean to sound so ungrateful for the rescue. I'm sure you've been searching for a while?"

He exhales loudly. "Oh, I've been searching. And over the last hour, I added a series of vague threats to my queries. If you thought we didn't have any allies on the train before, we're definitely vigilantes now."

We share an uncomfortable chuckle as he slips the key into our door and ushers me into the compartment.

Erick checks the adjoining door and confirms it's secure. "I'll lock this door behind me. For once, please follow instructions. Don't leave this compartment and don't open the door for anyone. Okay?"

"10-4, Sheriff."

His shoulders sag with exasperation. "I'll be back in five minutes with an ice pack, and then we're going to review our suspect list."

An attempt at a nod brings a swirl of pain inside my cranium. The rescue adrenaline masked the agony for a few minutes, but now the throbbing is intense. "Maybe you can scare up an aspirin too."

"I'll see what I can do." He exits the compartment and the tumblers scrape inside the lock as he secures me like a prisoner.

Locked in! I'm of much more use out there picking up vibes from the passengers. One pass through the restaurant car and I would most likely single out the guilty energy immediately.

Leaning forward to give chase, my vision swirls, and flashes of orange light blink around the perimeter.

Maybe I'll just wait for the ice. And after the swelling goes down, then I'll be better able to access my gifts.

The mood ring on my left hand circles an icy chill around my ring finger. Glancing down, an image of Pyewacket moves through the misty black dome.

No reception, Pye. I'd love to call you and see if you can shed any light on recent events, but I feel like this train is more of a time machine than a modern transportation device. They didn't have cell phones in the 1920s, and now you know why.

The image of Mr. Cuddlekins seems to nod in understanding. The feline fades and the mercurial mood ring returns to its normal state of indifference.

A key twists in the lock, and despite my inner knowing confirming that it's Erick, my chest tightens with residual fear.

"It's me, Mitzy." The door opens, and he steps through with a bag of ice cubes. "It's the best I could do."

"It's great. It'll be perfect." I reach for the bag and place it carefully over the tender lump on the back of my head. Now, I don't know if you've ever had to ice an injury, but it's not as soothing as people would lead you to believe. The ice is horribly cold, which causes both my hand and my head to ache in throbbing unison.

Erick opens the washstand cupboard and grabs a cloth.

"Here. Wrap the ice in this washcloth. It'll reduce the stinging a little. You need to keep that on your head for at least twenty minutes. And you really should not lie down, or fall asleep."

As I wrap the cotton cloth around the bag of ice, I scoff. "Good news. There's no chance of any of those things happening. This stabbing cold will absolutely keep me awake. And if I attempt to lie down, I think I might throw up."

Erick kneels next to me and shakes his head. "I'm going to run a concussion protocol on you, Moon." His expression turns serious and he fires questions at me.

"What train are we riding?"

"The Scenic Railway murder train."

He shakes his head and continues. "Whose murder are we solving?"

"Dame Joanna Hecht. But she's only an honorary 'dame.'"

"Who's your number one suspect at the moment?"

Tapping my finger on my lip, I hesitate. "Maybe Kevin Usher . . . That's not a hunch. He seems skeevy, and I'm sure he could swing a bat or whatever cracked my brain bucket."

He's not amused by my quip. "What time is it?"

I slide out my phone. "It's 3:04 p.m."

Erick tilts his head. "That's kind of cheating. How many days have we been on the train?"

"Technically?"

He nods.

"Barely one full day, but we boarded on Friday and now it's Saturday."

"What is the last thing you ate?"

I open my mouth, but nothing comes out. "I can't remember, but I don't think I liked it."

He holds one of his enticing fingers up in front of my face. Yes, I happen to think fingers can be appealing. No, it's not the head injury talking.

"I need you to follow my finger with your eyes. Don't move your head, only your eyes. Got it?"

"Yeah. I got smacked on the skull. I didn't get a lobotomy."

He moves his finger left and then slowly back to the right.

I follow it with my eyes. No big deal.

"Hmmmm. Let's try that one more time."

I don't like the tone of his voice. "All right. Go."

He moves his finger again, and holds it at the far edges a little longer than the first time.

"Well?" Adjusting the ice pack, I wait for his findings.

"Your eyes are jittering in both directions."

"And that means . . .?"

Failing to answer, he continues with the evaluation. "Go ahead and set that ice down for a minute. I need you to stand up." He demonstrates three balance poses with his hands resting on his hips: double leg, single leg, and tandem, and asks me to duplicate each one for twenty seconds, with my eyes closed.

I tip all over the place, open my eyes, and lift

my hands off my hips to grab the wall for support. "Did I pass?"

He nods and a sly grin creeps across his concerned face. "You got straight As in concussion. If that's what you're asking."

"Oh. I meant to ask, like, not having one."

"I gathered that. Unfortunately, you definitely have at least a mild concussion. We'll get you a CT scan when we get back to Pin Cherry. In the meantime, no extreme sports for you, and if that nausea gets any worse, I want to know about it right away."

His sincere concern is heartwarming. "I'll be all right, Erick. You worry too much."

He rocks back on his heels and looks up at me from his crouching position next to my legs. "I don't think it's possible to worry too much about you. I've never met anyone who has such a codependent relationship with danger."

"Rude." The pain in my head forces me to stifle the laughter. "Let's review the clues. I need some kind of distraction to take my mind off this ice torture."

Erick moves to the bench opposite and pulls a notepad out of his back pocket. "Ice torture. Anyone ever tell you that you have a flair for the dramatic, Moon?"

I shrug. "Almost everyone."

CHAPTER 10

ERICK IS STANDING guard outside the shower, while I wash the stink of steamer-trunk sweat and fear off my body. Knowing he's only a door's width away from my unclothed body, as I stand under the warm water and tenderly swish shampoo through my hair, is cause for a high level of preoccupation.

Not wanting to parade down the narrow passageway in a thin robe in the light of day, I chose to bring my change of clothing to the small shower stall.

Pre head injury, I could've managed with only minor difficulty, despite my clumsiness. However, now that my head is throbbing and my balance is tweaked, wedging myself into a clean pair of skinny jeans in such tight quarters is proving to be more difficult than fitting thirty-one clowns into a Volk-swagen bug.

A light knocking at the door. "You okay in there? Sounds like a struggle."

"Mind your own business, Sheriff. You're sup-posed to be guarding the door, not taking notes for the Foley artist."

He laughs louder than I would've expected. "That's a good one. Not many times you get an op-portunity to make a sound engineer joke."

While I'm impressed with his knowledge of the filmmaking industry, I'm not about to let him get an upper hand. "It wasn't a joke. Seriously, mind your own business. I'll be out in a minute."

He continues to chuckle at my predicament.

By the time I exit the facilities, my amused boyfriend has calmed himself, and I've come up with a plan of attack. "Why don't you interview the railway employees while I walk through the coach-class cars to see if anything jumps out?"

Erick wipes a strand of damp hair from my fore-head. "That's exactly what I'm afraid of."

"Wait? What?"

"I don't want anything jumping out at you. I think you've had enough excitement for one day."

"I appreciate your concern, but you said it your-self. The clock is ticking. One of my hunches is probably about the only thing that can save us at this point. If we don't figure out who the killer is before this train stops, the guilty party, and any remaining evidence, is going to walk right off this train and disappear."

"I can't argue with that, Moon. Stay in the bright, populated spaces. No more wandering off to the baggage car on your own. Deal?"

"Cross my heart and hope to—"

He presses a strong finger firmly over my lips. "I forbid you to finish that sentence."

My eyebrows rise and I pull my head back. "Forbid me? You should know better than to forbid me anything at this point, Sheriff."

He snickers, kisses me once, and shakes his head. "You'd think I would've learned my lesson, but it looks like I'm a glutton for punishment."

"That sounds a little like an insult. You consider me a punishment?"

"No. Never. The punishment is the emotional turmoil that caring for an independent woman causes me on a near daily basis."

"Oh, that. Well, you get what you pay for."

He walks toward our compartment, and his broad shoulders shake with laughter. "I don't know exactly what that means, but somehow it makes perfect sense."

I toss my dirty clothes and wet towel into the compartment, and Erick throws me some side eye.

He walks inside, scoops my wet towel from the floor, and hangs it on a hook. "Were you raised by wolves?"

His teasing tone amuses me, and I spout a hasty retort. "You'd think so, right?"

"Okay, I'm off to interview the employees, and you're going to walk tall in the aisles of the coach cars. If you find anything, your job is to come and get me. Please don't take matters into your own hands."

I pop a halfhearted salute and shrug in noncommittal agreement.

He groans and we part company.

The inaugural voyage of the refurbished train is full to the brim. At first glance, every seat seems to be taken.

Couples, families, a group of college students discussing philosophy and social injustice, and—

"Silas?"

The bald head and bulbous nose tip upward. "Good afternoon, Mizithra. How is your journey?"

The seat next to him and the two seats facing him are all empty. I collapse into one of them. "How are you on this train? I thought you were staying in Pin Cherry to take care of Pyewacket."

"I didn't want to raise an alarm, or cause you and the good sheriff to feel as though I was spying. My older brother is not well, and he requested a visit during our recently scheduled chat. Twiggy's taking care of all Robin Pyewacket Goodfellow's needs."

My mouth hangs open as though I'm a ventriloquist dummy with a broken mechanism.

Silas fills the silence with additional information. "My brother also enjoys a reputation as a renowned Latin scholar, and I felt his assistance in your grandmother's conundrum could prove fruitful."

Finally getting a hold of myself, I close my mouth and nod. "If there's any chance we can get Grams out of that infernal amber pendant, I'm all for it. I wish I'd known you were on the train! There's been an actual murder."

He leans forward, glances at the other passengers, and presses his finger to his lips. "Decorum."

"Sorry. Seeing you here threw me a little. Not to mention my concussion."

He harrumphs loudly and smooths his grey mustache with a thumb and forefinger. "Concussion?"

"Yeah. I've been helping Erick question passengers, and I must've made someone angry. I went into the baggage car and the next thing I knew somebody cracked me on the back of the head and shoved me into a trunk."

Without a verbal response, my mentor gets to

his feet and calmly places his left hand on the back of my head.

History has taught me to keep my mouth shut during these moments.

A strange tingling, that I can only describe as the sensation an injured bird must feel right before it regains the ability to fly, passes through my skull and into my grey matter.

"Better?"

I reach back, unable to find the enormous lump that once resided on the anterior of my noggin. "Fantastic. What did you do?"

His patronizing smile says it all.

"Understood. You transmuted something into something else and now my head's not throbbing. Thank you."

"Will you and the sheriff require assistance with this murder?"

"Not sure. We have some suspects and a working theory, but without an internet connection we haven't been able to follow up on any of our leads."

Silas steeples his fingers and his jowls wobble as he bounces his chin up and down on his pointer fingers. "What is the first problem?"

"I'm at least ninety-five percent sure that the victim was poisoned. Also pretty confident that the poison was put into her insulin. And that the killer had knowledge of the victim's condition and where her medicine would be kept."

He continues to bounce his chin without reply.

"But without access to the internet, I can't figure out what the poison is. Without knowing what type of poison, I can't really tie it to one of the passengers."

The bouncing stops abruptly. "Your gifts suffer the most when you trap yourself inside your mind. Close your eyes and describe the crime scene."

I do as I'm told. Walking Silas through events, from the scream that alerted us to the incident and the horrible perfume, I finish with our second examination of the body, which revealed the injection marks on the abdomen.

"Strong perfume and a healthy glow on the corpse, eh?" He rests his hands on his round belly and breathes in and out in a steady rhythm. "The potent scent of *eau de toilette* was likely used to mask the possible chemical odor some describe as similar to almond extract, while others describe it as a chlorine aroma. That, with the unusual pink lividity, indicates cyanide poisoning."

"Cyanide? You're sure?"

The milky-blue eyes of my alchemist/attorney seem to burrow into my mind. "I'm available to examine the body if you feel it is needed, but when have you known me to jest?"

"Fair point. Cyanide it is. I'll track down Erick and see if we can tie that to any of the first-class passengers."

"You're certain your killer is among them?"

"Not a hundred percent. But as sure as I can be with the information I have."

Before Silas can respond, my cell phone pings with multiple missed-call notifications.

"Reception! And I've missed a bunch of calls from Pyewacket. Hold that thought, Silas."

I move to the seat beside him and call my furry friend.

If cats can smile, then Pyewacket absolutely grins when he sees Silas next to me on screen. "What's up, son?" I return Pye's grin.

His tan skull dips out of frame, and only the black tufts of his ears are visible for a moment. When he comes back into view, he has a crinkled hunk of paper in his mouth.

"Back up a little. I can't quite make out the letters."

Silas leans toward my phone and a small exhale escapes. The scent of pipe tobacco is heavy on his breath, and I wonder if he stepped out to the viewing car to have a puff. "What is it? Do you recognize it?"

He nods. "Unless I am severely mistaken, that is

the crinkled outer wrapper from a stick of Doublemint chewing gum."

Leaning toward my phone, I can finally see part of the letters within the black bar on the bright-green background. "Oh, I see it now."

Pyewacket drops the paper and grooms his magnificent whiskers with his left paw. The scars over his eye are more visible in the harsh light of the video conferencing setup. I wonder— Best not to let myself get distracted. "A gum wrapper. I don't get it, Pye."

Silas strokes his mustache and his eyes wander off, deep in thought, while I continue to question the cat.

"Does the killer chew gum? By the way, you were right about the poison. Definitely has to be the cause of death."

Pyewacket's eyelids lazily squeeze closed. "Reeow." Soft but condescending.

"Easy, smarty paws. Gum? I got nothing. Am I looking for someone who manufactures gum, someone who's trying to quit smoking by chewing gum? There are too many options."

Silas slowly rolls his head against the headrest and turns toward me. "Doublemint gum. Wasn't their slogan—?"

"Twins! How could I not get that immediately? The Doublemint twins lived in Sedona! Maybe

Pyewacket is trying to tell us there's some duplicity involved? Maybe Joanna and Alice aren't just sisters, maybe they're twins!"

Silas has no idea what I'm talking about, but nods his encouragement regardless.

The screen jitters and the call is lost.

"Shoot! I didn't even get to say hi to Grams. Do you really think your brother can help?"

"I do. I hate to say it is my last resort, but I've been consumed by research for weeks. No solution has presented itself. If Jedediah cannot find a light in these paths of darkness"—he pats his satchel, and I assume it contains the sacred tome *Loca Sine Lumine, Loca Sine Lege*—"then I fear your grandmother must choose an eternity in a necklace, or a one-way ticket to the other side."

We commiserate in silence, as the clickety-clacking whir of the train hums between us.

"I better get back to Erick. After this morning's antics, he's a little wound up. I'll let him know about Mr. Cuddlekins' latest clue and the cyanide thing. Hopefully, that will lead us to someone before the train stops."

Silas raises his bushy grey eyebrows. "Yes, you must apprehend the guilty before they have the opportunity to flee. I'm sure you and Mr. Harper are the right team for the job."

"Thanks for the vote of confidence." Without

permission, I lean over and kiss his ruddy cheek. "Thank you for doing everything you can to set Grams free. You're the best."

He blushes and shakes his head. "You only have three hours to corral the crook, Mizithra."

"Copy that."

Armed with a clean sweep of the passenger cars, I return to first class to find Erick.

He's exchanging pleasantries in the bar car with Mlle. Lenormand, and her fawning expression raises my hackles.

I slip an arm around his waist and squeeze. "Hi, sweetie. Did you want to join me for a drink and a snack?"

He's no dummy, but he is a professional. He bites the edge of his lip to keep from grinning and makes his excuses with the phony psychic.

"If I didn't know better, Moon, I'd say you're jealous."

"Who? Me? Not even a little. I didn't want her to get any of her divine glitter on your snazzy flannel shirt."

He nearly doubles over with laughter as he walks toward sustenance. "Snazzy and flannel in the same sentence. You've outdone yourself." He pulls out a chair for me, and I eagerly dive into the happy-hour menu.

"Will the two of you be starting a tab?"

My eyes must light up too quickly.

Erick shakes his head. "Just water for us."

The server bows her head and shuffles away.

"You seem awfully chipper for a concussed woman." He tilts his head.

"I'm a fast healer." No need to out my alchemical savior. "So, do you want to know what I uncovered during my search?"

Setting his menu on the cranberry damask tablecloth, he holds up his hand. "First, the order. Let's split the venison sliders, and I'll get you an order of fries while I tackle an onion blossom. Sound good?"

"It's like you read my mind."

He places our order when the server returns with the waters, and gestures for me to tell my story as he quenches his thirst.

"Dame Joanna died of cyanide poisoning."

He sputters a little, sets down his glass, and wipes his chin with the back of his hand. "That's some hunch. A quick stroll through coach class, and you've somehow conducted a postmortem."

Basking in the glow for a moment, I opt to spill a few of the beans. "I wish I could take the credit. Truth is, I bumped into Silas Willoughby, and when I described the crime scene, he identified the toxin immediately."

Erick smiles and nods. "Now *that* I believe. But what is he doing on the train?"

"He's off to visit his sick brother. He changes trains in Sault Ste. Marie. Apparently, he didn't want us to think he was spying, so he opted to travel on the down low."

Nodding, he chews the inside of his cheek. "What makes him so sure it was cyanide?"

I explain the stinky perfume masking the almond-esque odor, and the bit about the bright pink skin.

"Makes sense. If I could've managed a second of internet access, I might've figured it out on my own."

"Ooooo. Speaking of internet. There was a flash of connectivity, and when I called the bookshop, Pyewacket held up a gum wrapper."

Erick leans forward on his elbows and whispers, "Wow. Looks like the case is pretty much solved."

"Don't get smart, Sheriff. It was a Doublemint gum wrapper. You know, 'Double your pleasure.' The twins! I think Joanna and Alice were twins. Maybe the victim is really Alice, and Joanna pretended to kill herself because she's running from a deep, dark secret."

He rubs a hand across his forehead and eyes. "You definitely watch way too many movies."

"Truth is stranger than fiction. I think we

should at least entertain it as a possibility." Crossing my arms over my chest, I offer a pouty scowl.

His head rolls from side to side. "Fine. We'll entertain it. I think we'll get a lot further if we can figure out who has access to cyanide."

"Or has the knowledge to make it themselves."

He shakes his head. "Not that it's as complicated as splitting an atom, but do you really think someone extracted this on their own?"

The food arrives, and I shove a few french fries into my mouth before responding. "Think about it. Buying cyanide wouldn't be easy. A credit card could be tracked, and even if you paid cash, there can't be many suppliers. Extracting it from apricot kernels in the privacy of your own home is about the only way you could cover your tracks."

A scowl flashes across his handsome face. "The Josephs own orchards, right?"

Biting my bottom lip, I nod slowly. "Sure, but they don't have a motive—do they? The possible twin angle. Money. Dark family secrets. That's the stuff that could bring out the killer in the common man, or woman, I suppose."

Munching thoughtfully on a fried onion petal, he nods. "You're a dangerous enigma, Moon. Remind me never to make you angry."

With a setup like that, how can I resist? "You wouldn't like me when I'm angry."

Thankfully, he gets my *Incredible Hulk* joke, and we share a chuckle.

After polishing off our venison sliders, I finish my fries and lick the salt from my fingers. "What's our next move?"

"Let's talk to Alice. If she and Joanna were twins, I think the two of us can pry that out of her at some point." He winks.

Returning the wink, I tap my fingertips together like a cartoon villain. "Excellent."

Erick signs for our meal as I anxiously pace near the exit. We're about to solve this case with time to spare.

His firm knock on Alice's compartment speaks of experience.

"Who is it?" Her voice is rife with contempt.

"It's Sheriff Harper, ma'am. I have a few more questions."

An irritated scoff filters through the door. She waves us in and scowls in my direction. "Be brief. I have arrangements to attend to."

Positioning myself to get the best view of, and vibes from, the suspect, I let Erick take the lead on the interrogation.

"Alice, what's the age difference between you and your sister?"

Her jaw tightens and her eyebrows arch. "Not

that it has any bearing on this case, but Joanna was seven years older."

He nods. "So you weren't twins?"

She leans away from him in shock. "I should say not. Joanna looks at least a decade older than me. She never took care of herself."

"How long had she been suffering from diabetes?"

Genuine concern replaces the shock. "It came on quite suddenly in her twenties."

"Was there some change in her lifestyle or health habits?"

Alice looks out the window, and my extrasensory perceptions feel the heat of a deeply buried secret. I knew it!

"I suppose she drank a bit more after her husband passed. She was never the same. Hers was that rare true love people are always going on about."

Interesting deflection. There's something beneath it. No longer able to contain myself, I leap into the fray. "For a couple so deeply in love, you would think they'd have had children. Did Joanna have children?"

"Joanna was unable to conceive."

Another swerve. The question I asked could've been answered by a simple yes or no, but Alice chose to rephrase and qualify. I'm sure Erick recognized it, even without the benefit of psychic senses.

I press her further. "Many couples who can't conceive turn to adoption. Did Joanna and her husband adopt?"

The clairsentient wash of guilt that emanates from Alice is so powerful, I wonder if it's visible to the naked eye.

Erick definitely picks up on the shift. "Alice, it seems like you're keeping something from us. Did Joanna adopt?"

When she turns her head away from the window and looks at him, her eyes are brimming with tears. "A girl."

"What happened to the child? Was she killed in the same accident that took Joanna's husband?"

Alice shakes her head vigorously and tears roll down her cheeks.

Opening her washstand cupboard, I grab a tissue and hand it to her.

"Thank you. The sudden loss of her husband destroyed her. She couldn't care for the girl, and I was in no position—"

Erick's jaw tenses. "Alice, what happened to the girl?"

"Joanna sent her back."

"Back to where?"

Alice sobs into the tissue, and I grab two more to thrust in her direction. She sops up the tears and snot, and takes a ragged breath. "We had to send the girl back to the orphanage. Nothing could be done. It was the best thing for her."

"What year was this?"

Alice dabs at her eyes. "I'm not exactly sure. It would've been over twenty-five years ago, at least. I've worked hard to push those images from my mind."

"And how old was the girl?"

I think I can see where Erick is going with this.

"She was sent back just before her sixth birthday."

"So she'd be in her early thirties now?"

The distraught woman shrugs. "I suppose."

"Did you or Joanna ever hear from the girl, or the orphanage, again?"

She sighs heavily. "There was an incident about ten years later. Joanna received a letter from the girls. They ask for employment in her household. Promising to work for free if she would just get them out of the orphanage."

Erick looks at me and arches one eyebrow. "Them? I thought she only adopted one girl?"

A new wave of sobs racks Alice's body. "Joanna could be quite stubborn. She only wanted one child. Just that one."

My mood ring fires to life and the image of the gum wrapper flashes through the mists. "Twins.

They were twins, but your sister only adopted one of them."

Alice nods until it looks as though her head will fall from her shoulders. As I lean forward to comfort her, an emphatic cry echoes down the passageway.

"Help! Someone fetch a doctor! Hurry!"

Erick jumps up, opens the door, and looks toward the sound.

Alice buries her face in her hands and makes no effort to follow us as we exit her compartment.

In the passageway near 4B, Lulu Weathers is convulsing.

CHAPTER 11

Before Erick dives in to play the role of the knight in shining armor, that comes so naturally to him, he turns to me and whispers, "This could be a second victim of the poisoner. Let's not say anything until we have more information."

"Understood." I can't believe he assumed I would blurt. I mean, I absolutely would've blurted, but it's rather cheeky of him to assume.

He rushes down the passageway, calmly taking control. "I need everyone to step away from Mrs. Weathers.

"You: find a porter or the conductor and ask them to get Sheriff Harper oxygen and a mask.

"You: get me someone on the cleaning staff and tell them to bring two sets of thick rubber gloves.

"You: move these people back."

As the various individuals he's commanded stumble off to do his bidding, he rolls Lulu onto her left side. I won't get into the details of what happens next. Suffice to say that his decisive action prevented asphyxiation. There's an old sixties song about "what goes up must come down." This is pretty much the opposite of that. I turn away to prevent my own gag reflex from joining the party. However, I can't ignore the hint of almond extract tinged with chemical cherry that wafts upward.

"Mrs. Weathers, it's Sheriff Harper. Are you able to respond?"

No response.

Erick looks over his shoulder. "Mitzy, check the room. This looks like ingestion rather than—"

He's thinking injection. He doesn't have to say it. "Copy that." Averting my gaze, I slip behind him and into Lulu's room.

Two pairs of flats are carefully aligned at the end of one bench. Her hand towel is perfectly folded in thirds and hangs at the very center of her towel rack inside the washstand. Her minimal toiletries are aligned a finger-width apart on the left side of the faucet. She must be a meticulous person.

A quick peek in her closet reveals four outfits on hangers, equally spaced on the utilitarian bar.

With such precision in her character, it's easy for me to identify what's out of place. The hardcover book sprawled on the carpet, in between the benches, was obviously not placed there by Mrs. Weathers.

The saucer on the bench seat and the tipped teacup, still dripping its contents onto the cushion, are also clear indications of foul play.

Walking toward the teacup, I bend and my hand hovers near the handle—

"Don't touch that!" Erick's sudden shout sends a jolt of fear through my body.

"It's spilling tea on—"

He looks at me and clenches his jaw. "Remember what we talked about?"

"You mean the— Right. This could be— No touching. Got it." Erick is telling me, without words, how cyanide can be absorbed through the skin.

The various directives he issued are coming to fruition, and he turns to attend to them.

He slips the thick rubber gloves on his hands, but continues to maintain a healthy distance from the puddle around Lulu's head.

I suppose my only job is to make sure no one touches the tainted teacup. Crossing my arms, I observe his careful conduct.

He addresses the janitor. "We need to clean this up as quickly as possible. Put on some gloves, like these, and make sure none of this comes in contact with your skin. And wear a mask. It could be contagious."

The custodian nods and suits up.

How clever of Erick. "Contagious" carries enough information to keep people away from the spill, without causing the alarm that "poisonous" would've generated. That gorgeous man is easily as smart as he looks.

"Do you have a plastic bag in your kit?" He gestures toward the custodian's case.

The man with the cleaning supplies nods, and Erick points to me. "Give it to her, please."

I take the offered bag, turn it inside out, and scoop the teacup and saucer inside without coming in contact with any of the spilled liquid. Tying a knot at the top of the bag, I wait for further instructions.

"I need to get her in the shower and rinse this off to prevent re-contamination. Can you wait here, collect a sample, and make sure this is all cleaned up properly?"

I nod. I'm not super psyched about collecting a "sample" of the—I can't even think it, but I'm trying to be a cooperative girlfriend and honorary deputy. That last bit I've awarded myself. I mean, I'm doing all the work of a deputy, so why not include an imaginary badge?

"Thanks, Moon. Try to find her a change of clothes, and when the oxygen arrives let me know."

"Will do."

Erick awkwardly drags Mrs. Weathers down the hallway toward the shower stall at the end of the car, careful to prevent cross-contamination.

The area outside 4B is meticulously cleaned with lemon-scented products, and, as far as I can tell, the janitor takes all the necessary precautions. When he finishes, I place a towel on the clean bench and select some dry clothes for Lulu. Bundling them up, I tuck the packet under my arm and wait for the oxygen.

I hope we got to her fast enough. I know next to nothing about cyanide poisoning, but I'll cross my fingers that her inability to keep the tea down and Erick's rapid washing of her skin and clothes will be enough to save her life.

A porter arrives with a small oxygen tank, connection tubes, and a sterile mask, still in its packaging. "Did you request the oxygen, ma'am?"

"No. It was Sheriff Harper. There's an emergency. Follow me."

Pulling Lulu's door closed behind me, I lead the way to the shower.

Erick left the door open and he's holding Mrs. Weathers, still fully clothed, under the direct spray.

"The oxygen's here. Were you able to get her rinsed off in time?"

His hair and shirt are wet. His blond bangs hang messily across his face. "I hope so. Can you hand me that towel?"

I hand him a large cream towel and he wraps it tightly around Lulu. "We have to take her back to our compartment." His eyes say "I'm sorry," but his decisive actions make no apology.

He carries her toward our accommodations, and I gesture for the porter to follow.

"Place a couple more towels down, Mitzy. We need to get that oxygen in her right away."

I drop the bundle of her dry things on the opposite bench and lay two of our towels down as fast as I can.

Erick gently places her on the covered bench and reaches for the oxygen. He rips open the mask and tubing, and connects everything up like a pro. Once the oxygen is flowing, he places the mask over Lulu's nose and mouth and secures the strap over her head.

"Mrs. Weathers, I need you to breathe. Try to breathe as deeply as you can. You need to get as much oxygen into your lungs as possible." He props her up with a bolster and looks up at me with barely a glimmer of hope in his eyes. "You can help her into her dry clothes if she regains consciousness."

"If? Don't you think you got to her in time?"

"It's difficult to say. We don't know how much she ingested. I suppose it's good that she got some of it out of her system. I don't have an antidote kit, but I'll make sure they call ahead to have an ambulance waiting with one at the depot."

The porter stands meekly in the doorway, looking back and forth between Erick and me. "Is it contagious?"

Sheriff Harper assumes an authoritative pose. "For now, let's assume that it is. Make sure no one goes into her compartment. No cleaning staff, no other porters—no one. Understood?"

The small man nods. "Will there be anything else?" He is already stepping backward, and a clear wave of relief washes over him when Erick shakes his head.

"What possible motive would someone have to murder a minister?"

Erick runs a thumb along his jawline. "I think we better lock down everyone's alibis as soon as we can. Do you think it would be possible to ask Mr. Willoughby to sit in our compartment and make sure there's not a second attempt on her life, while we conduct the interviews?"

"I'm sure he'll help. Should I go check? Of course I should. I'll go right now."

He nods and stands guard as I turn to leave.

Thankfully, he pretends not to notice when I bang into the door that the porter closed as he scurried off. Opening the door in silent embarrassment, I make haste to the passenger cars.

Not only is Silas willing to comply with Erick's request, but also he's certain he has a tincture or powder tucked somewhere in his mysterious tweed jacket that will restore Mrs. Weathers.

The thought hadn't even occurred to me, but I'm pleased that serendipity is on our side.

Silas takes up his sentry post, offers me a reassuring wink, and we head out to catch a killer.

Gripping Erick's elbow, I pull him close in the passageway outside the compartment.

He quickly kisses my forehead. "I'm sorry our getaway has been derailed. No pun intended."

"Me too. But that's not what's bothering me."

"Something's bothering you?" He bends toward me, concern clouding his handsome face.

"Um, yeah. Remember that trunk I was in?"

He leans away and scrunches up his face as though I must be crazy. "Let me think. Do I remember using a fire axe to smash through the lock of the trunk inside which my girlfriend was trapped? Hmmmm. It's not ringing a bell."

Playfully punching him in the stomach, I shake my head. "That's not what I meant. I mean, what's a human-sized empty trunk doing on a train?"

The humor rapidly fades from his face and is replaced by suspicion. "Good point. Although, the porter did offer to store our bags in the baggage compartment once we unpacked. Do you think someone just brought that much stuff?"

Now it's my turn to make a joke. "If we were traveling with my grandmother, I'd say absolutely. But in this day and age, it seems unlikely that anyone besides Mrs. Howell would pack a massive trunk for such a brief excursion."

He ignores my *Gilligan's Island* reference and licks his lip. For a moment, I'm mesmerized by the subtle sheen on his kissable mouth. "Did I lose you, Moon?"

My cheeks flush. "You wish."

In a remarkable moment of synchronicity, we both shout, "The body!"

Lifting my hands in celebration, I nod my head. "I know, right? Maybe the killer planned to stuff Dame Joanna's body in that trunk, and Alice just happened to discover her before they had the chance."

He nods briefly. "Possibly. But how did they plan to get the trunk into Dame Joanna's compartment and then move the body-filled trunk back to the baggage car?"

The sheriff has a point. Lugging a huge trunk through first class would draw some attention.

"What if they planned on putting her in there before she died?"

A shiver passes through my body and Erick puts an arm around my shoulders. "You think maybe they messed up the dosage of the poison?"

My head bobs enthusiastically. "What if they planned to walk her back to the baggage car while the poison was taking effect, but she was sicker than they thought and she died too quickly?"

He leans against the elegant lacquered wood framing the train's window, and his silence must mean he's playing out the various options. "I don't know, Mitzy. It seems awfully risky. It's a long walk from 2B to the baggage car. Anyone could've seen them."

Biting my bottom lip, I nod in agreement. "True. I was wandering around looking for snacks. They could've run into any number of people. It's not a very sneaky plan." I gaze out the window, hoping the glistening waves or my reticent ring will offer some additional information.

Blimey!

My mood ring burns to life. Glancing down, I see rapid flashes of costumed performers and death-defying acrobatics.

There certainly must be a cartoon lightbulb popping on above my head. I grip Erick's arm and gasp. "Maybe the trunk wasn't a way out; maybe it was the way in!"

"The way in? What are you talking about?"

"Maybe there's someone who isn't on the passenger manifest, because they didn't *walk* on board."

The same comic-strip lightbulb clicks to life above his head, and he nods slowly. "It wouldn't be the easiest way onto the train, but you were able to fit in there."

"I'm not sure if that's a compliment or an insult. Are you saying I must be incredibly flexible and tiny, or are you saying the trunk was clearly large enough to fit anyone?"

His tantalizing blue eyes sparkle and he presses his lips together to keep from chuckling. "The first one, obviously."

Shaking my head, I push him down the passageway in front of me. "Let's start with Margo, Kevin, and the elusive Orson. Those are the three weasels I suspect."

We're halfway through the "B" train when Erick slips a paper out of his front pocket and calls out their compartment numbers. "3A, 4A, 4C."

Sadly, Kevin Usher is our first stop. I wisely position myself behind my six-foot-and-change boyfriend.

"Well, if it isn't the lawman and his smart-mouthed sidekick."

Erick lays a firm hand on Kevin's chest and pushes him backward with just the right amount of force to be intimidating, but not cross the line. "The only thing I want to hear coming out of your mouth, Mr. Usher, is an explanation of where you were, at 2:00 a.m. this morning?"

Kevin's upper lip curls. "I was here, in my compartment."

A strange tingling lifts the hairs on the back of my neck. "Were you alone?"

He clears his throat and looks directly at me. "You already tired of this one, toots?" He jerks his thumb toward Erick.

Once again, Sheriff Harper places his hand on Kevin's chest, and this time he presses him against the wall—firmly. "Answer the nice lady's question, Mr. Usher."

"Easy, man. I've got my hands full of dames already." Kevin snickers. "I'm seldom alone. So if you want a piece of the Usher, you better take a number." He leers in my direction.

Erick scoffs, but I laugh out loud. "I don't see a

line, *Kev*. But if there were a line, I can guarantee you I wouldn't be caught dead in it."

A quick flash of pride and satisfaction from my beau ruffles my extrasensory perceptions, and Erick picks up the interrogation. "Who was in your compartment?"

Kevin smiles defiantly. "That gypsy fortune teller, Lenore something or other. She was here for a while, too. I probably told her fortune two or three times."

My skin tries to crawl away. Yuck and yuck. "And where were you an hour ago?"

"In the bar car having afternoon tea."

I'm not sure if Erick can smell the *tea*, but I'm inclined to believe Mr. Usher's disgusting alibis.

Sheriff Harper steps back, fixes Kevin's collar, and pats him patronizingly on the cheek. "It'll be easy enough to check those alibis. Might be a good idea for you to stay in your compartment until we reach the next stop. I'll make sure the porter brings you some supper."

Mr. Usher opens his mouth to protest, but Erick squares his shoulders and looks down at the man with that "high noon at the O.K. Corral" stare.

Kevin's Adam's apple struggles to accommodate a swallow. "Sure thing. Sure."

We slip out and move toward Margo's compartment.

When we see the porter enter the car, Erick informs him that Mr. Usher has requested his supper be delivered at seven.

The porter nods and makes a note on his pad.

A quick knock on Margo's door reveals her in red-satin loungewear, with a bottle of champagne on ice.

She outwardly keeps her cool, but I sense more than a passing shock to find us at her door. "Who were you expecting, Margo?"

"What? What makes you think I was expecting someone?" She bats her lashes and looks away.

Erick casually points to the champagne and the pair of flutes.

She shrugs. "Oh, that. I may have invited someone to stop in for a chat, but clearly they had other plans." Her sentence ends with the palpable sting of bitterness.

"Ms. Powell, where were you at 2:00 a.m. this morning?" He crosses his arms and waits.

She repeats her pathetically rehearsed story about noise-canceling headphones and audiobooks.

Erick doesn't take the bait. "I've questioned a lot of suspects in my day, and absolutely none of what you said rings true. Where were you?"

She drops onto the expertly upholstered bench and pours herself a glass of champagne. "I was working on a story."

Sheriff Harper shakes his head. "We both know you're retired."

She flutters her gaudy fingernails and smirks. "A reputable journalist is never completely retired. I'm freelancing now. One big story could land me a talk show contract. And the right story might see me through a five-year gig and syndication deals."

I've had about enough of this woman. "Suit yourself, Margo. I just thought I should let you know, we're on our way to question Orson Elliott."

Bingo!

Not even a practiced fabricator of falsehoods like her had time to adjust her body language. Whatever she was doing in the wee hours of the morning, and whatever plans she has right now, have everything to do with Orson Elliott.

"I promised him a fifteen hundred word review."

Kicking out a hip, I scoff. "Where? In your diary?"

She nearly spills her champagne. "How dare you? I still have connections. I won three daytime Emmys."

"We can play this game all day, Margo." I roll my eyes. "What do you think Mr. Elliott is going to tell us?"

All the hot air hisses out of her over-inflated ego. "I may have told him I was a literary critic for a large newspaper." She guzzles the rest of her bubbly and sighs. "Clearly he was more interested in the publicity than the person."

Erick steps in to ask the more risqué questions. "And what did he offer you in exchange for your glowing review in this imaginary paper?"

Her shoulders droop and she exhales. "Sex. It's always about sex or money. Right?"

He avoids responding. "So your alibi for this morning at 2:00 a.m. is that you were in Orson's compartment? Or was he here?"

She rolls her head back-and-forth in exasperation. "He was here. He was here all night. I could barely shove him out with a crowbar this morning."

"Thank you for your cooperation, Ms. Powell. Once we confirm your alibi with Mr. Elliott, I think we can safely remove you from the suspect list. Now, where were you an hour ago?"

She gestures to herself from head to polished toes. "I'm a mature woman, Sheriff. It takes a while to look this good. I was here in my compartment. As if that weren't obvious."

The glug, glug, glug of champagne gushing from the bottle as she refills her glass resounds in the tight quarters.

I gently touch Erick's back, and when he looks at me, I nod. We step out of her room and head off in search of Orson.

CHAPTER 12

"LET'S CHECK IN with Silas and see how Lulu's doing." I gesture toward our compartment as we make our way down the narrow passage in the "C" sleeping car.

Erick knocks lightly on the door.

The surprisingly rough voice of Mr. Willoughby replies. "Who goes there?"

"It's just me and Erick, Silas."

He harrumphs. "Come in. Come in."

The door opens hesitantly and we step in. I freeze in my tracks at the sight of an alert and lucid Lulu Weathers. "Wow. Are you all right?"

Silas replies on her behalf. "Sheriff Harper's quick intervention greatly reduced Mrs. Weathers' exposure. She will certainly be delicate for a couple of days, but the vast majority of the poison never had an opportunity to take effect. I would counsel seeking medical attention in Sault Ste. Marie, but I believe Mrs. Weathers will make a full recovery."

A faint twinkle in his eye catches my attention, and I know without asking that one of his alchemical solutions deserves all the credit for saving Lulu's life.

Erick steps forward. "Did you see the person who poisoned your tea?"

She looks away and mumbles.

"Sorry, Mrs. Weathers, I couldn't hear you. Did you know the person?"

She gazes out the window and the reply seems to take a great effort. "At lunch, I asked my waiter if I could have a cup of tea delivered to my compartment. He said it would be no problem. There was a knock at my door, I opened it, and a porter handed me the saucer and teacup."

Silas clears his throat. "How odd. Generally, tea is delivered on a tray, with the teapot, cream, sugar, and a selection of tea options."

I don't know that much about tea service, but if Silas says it should be delivered on a tray, I'm inclined to believe him. "Did you recognize the porter?"

Her eyes dart to my face briefly, before returning to the scenery slipping by outside the window. "I'm ashamed to say, I barely looked. And what's worse, I didn't have any cash. So I didn't even tip the poor fellow."

"But you're certain it was a male porter?"

The question seems to throw her for a moment and she rubs her left thumb on her right arm with such force it leaves a red mark. "I don't know. I— I think it was. They smelled a little like cedar."

"Lulu, were you feeling all right before the tea was delivered?"

She exhales and leans back against the seat.

At this point, I notice she's changed into dry clothing. "Silas, did you help her change?"

Silas lifts his bushy eyebrows in shock. "Under no circumstances. Highly inappropriate. When Mrs. Weathers was feeling up to it, I stepped into the passageway to allow her the privacy to get out of her wet things."

Lulu rolls her head toward me and a wan smile lifts her cheeks. "Thank you for leaving me that bundle of clothes, Mitzy."

I step forward and sit next to her on the bench. "What's wrong? If I didn't know better, I'd think you were lying to us. Ministers don't lie, do they?" Despite my personal opinion on dishonesty being an equal opportunity offender, I ask the leading question to ply her with guilt.

She exhales dramatically and drops her face

into her hands. "I'm so ashamed. I know the Lord will forgive me, but I may never forgive myself."

"Mrs. Weathers, if you have any information pertinent to this case, you must share it. This is a murder investigation, and there can be serious charges for impeding it." Erick's voice has a hard edge, and I know he's frustrated with all the deception that's stalling our investigation.

Without lifting her head, Lulu confesses her sins. "Early this morning, I did hear a noise. I opened the door of my room, just a crack, and I saw someone leaving Dame Joanna's compartment. It was dark, and I wasn't sure. I didn't want to make any false accusations, but—"

"Who did you see?" Erick's tone is stern with an edge of threat.

She swallows audibly. "I can't be sure. It was dark—"

I gently place my hand on her knee. "Lulu, it wasn't that dark. The moon was nearly full, and the train was running right along the shoreline. The reflection off the water was easily enough for at least a rough description. Tell us what you saw."

A rough sob catches in her throat. "They saw me. They saw me and that's why they came after me. If I say something, they'll try again."

Erick widens his stance. "Mrs. Weathers, this train is going to stop in less than two hours. If you don't help us apprehend this murderer, they'll walk free. Free to kill you or anyone else."

She laces her fingers in a prayerful pose. "Vengeance is mine, saith the Lord."

Without missing a beat Erick replies, "Thou shalt not kill."

Lulu swipes at her tears with the back of her hand. "It was a man. He was small statured, but I'm sure it was a man. I didn't get a good look at his face. I think there was a mustache, but no beard. I don't know. Maybe I'm imagining it."

Squeezing her knee encouragingly, I nod. "And you're sure that he saw you?"

"Not me exactly, but he saw me close my door. It's not hard to figure out who's in which compartment."

I pat her leg, stand, and whisper to Erick. "Either he stopped the porter in the passageway and slipped the poison into the tea, or he disguised himself as a porter and delivered the tea himself."

Erick shifts his weight back and forth on his feet. "A porter's key, a porter with poisoned tea . . . Maybe our killer isn't a passenger.

"Mrs. Weathers, would you recognize the porter who delivered your tea in a lineup?" Erick crosses his arms and taps his toe.

Lulu shakes her head. "I don't think so. I'd be

guessing. I don't want my guess to condemn someone."

Silas smooths his mustache with thumb and forefinger, and catches my eye.

The wordless missive hits home. "Hey, why don't you see what you can find out about the porters, Erick? Work history, anybody new . . . stuff like that. I'll see if I can help Lulu remember any other details."

He exhales loudly. "All I can hear is the clock ticking, Moon. I'm not about to let this guy commit a homicide, plus an attempted murder, and walk away free."

"We'll catch him. Don't worry. We got this."

Erick leaves the compartment with a huff and a shake of his head.

Silas mumbles something under his breath as his fingers trace symbols in the air.

Lulu's head tilts against the window and she falls into a deep sleep.

My mentor pats the seat next to him, and I join without question.

"Mizithra, there is an illusion at work."

"Magic? Are you saying someone is using magic on the train?"

His mustache sags with disappointment as I misinterpret his message. "Hardly. In my experience, women tend to choose poison. However, your eyewitness has given evidence to lead us in a different direction. What do you see?"

I know he's asking about my psychic information, but it hasn't been entirely helpful. I fill him in on the interviews and alibis we collected, remind him of Pyewacket's clues, and mention the acrobatic vision in my ring.

"You were placed in a large empty trunk. I agree that it would've held far too much baggage for your average traveler. However, what if *twin* is too literal? What if the duplicitousness is of a more subtle variety? Two would need significantly more luggage than one."

At first the riddle confuses me, but slowly a light creeps in. "*Victor/Victoria?*"

Silas grins broadly. "Ah, the angelic voice of Julie Andrews. Will there ever be another?"

Considering his slim knowledge of pop culture, I'm honestly a little thrown that he got my reference. "So you're saying, maybe the twin isn't a literal identical twin. Maybe it's one person being two people. Is it a man dressed as a woman or a woman dressed as a man?"

"Seems you've had difficulty locating this Orson Elliott passenger. Perhaps more effort must be made."

Armed with a new theory and a boost of energy, I hop up and head for the door. "When

Erick gets back, let him know I went to question Orson."

Silas harrumphs. "That hardly seems wise, Mizithra. If this person is the poisoner, or connected to the poisoner, approaching him alone holds dangerous consequences."

"I'll be fine. We both know I'm going in with my eyes open. I'll be on guard. It's hard to surprise someone when they're already expecting the worst, right?"

Silas digs around inside the hidden pockets of his tattered tweed coat and retrieves a small vial of brown liquid. "Take this just in case. If you believe yourself to have been poisoned, drink this immediately. Do not hesitate. Do not doubt your instincts. I will inform the sheriff of your foolhardy venture the moment he arrives."

Slipping the vial in the pocket of my jeans, I nod and close the compartment door quietly behind me.

The passageway is empty as I approach Orson's room, located next to ours.

KNOCK. KNOCK. KNOCK.

Strong, but not threatening. A knock that carries authority and demands a response.

No response is offered.

Glancing up and down the passageway, I decide to risk it. The lock is simple enough to pick, and fortunately I open the door to find the compartment empty. I close the varnished wooden door behind me and lock it to buy a little extra time.

The washstand contains gender-neutral cleaning supplies, and there are no telltale items lying in the open.

When I open the closet a distinct aroma hits me head on. Instantly, I flash back to being trapped in the trunk. Stumbling back, I take a few deep breaths and attempt to return to my search. Wait. That smell . . .

Cedar! Like an old hope chest. Lulu said something about the porter smelling like cedar. Bingo! My regular, and my super, senses confirm that I'm on the right track.

The room may offer little in the way of clues, but the closet tells a fascinating story. Complete wardrobes, for male and female characters, as well as a remarkable replica of Mlle. Lenormand's caftan and headpiece.

We're dealing with a master of disguise.

There are men's and women's shoes, various faux facial hairpieces, wigs, a cane . . . It would be impressive if it weren't so dastardly.

Footsteps outside the door send a chill through my blood, and there's nowhere to hide.

The connecting door! I tap in panicked staccato at the door between the adjoining compartments.

Hopefully Silas will hear me and I can slip away undiscovered.

No response.

The key is in the lock. Orson Elliott, or whoever he is, will be inside this compartment in seconds. Knocking with more desperation, the key clicks and I prepare for the worst.

"Mr. Elliott, do you have a moment?"

Once again, Erick saves me! His authoritative voice fills the outer passageway and stops Orson in his tracks.

The door between the compartments pops open. Silas pulls me through with surprising force and secures the door behind me.

Lulu is still sleeping soundly in her alchemical world of healing.

I press my ear to the door of my compartment and eavesdrop on Erick's interrogation. "So it's your statement that you did not spend the night in Margo Powell's room?"

Mr. Elliott's voice carries a faint Russian accent, and he confirms Erick's recap.

"So where were you at 2:00 a.m. this morning, Mr. Elliott?"

"Asleep, as I'm sure were you."

"And about an hour ago? Can you account for your whereabouts?"

"It's a scenic train, no? I walk. I see this scenery."

"Can anyone vouch for your whereabouts?"

The accent thickens with frustration. "How do I know this? I don't plan my day for alibis."

"Well, you be careful, Mr. Elliott. There's definitely a murderer loose on the train."

I place a hand over my mouth and my eyes widen. That's wholly out of character for Erick to say something like that to a passenger. He must suspect Orson. I think it might be time to apply some additional pressure to Mr. Elliott's carefully constructed façade.

Opening the door of our compartment, I step into the hallway and revel in the shock that ripples across Orson's features. "Oh, excuse me, Erick, do you have a minute?"

CHAPTER 13

MR. ELLIOTT USES the distraction to his advantage and ducks into his compartment.

Erick lunges forward, but I catch his elbow and shake my head. "Come with me."

He stands his ground for a moment and looks at Orson's closed door with irritation pinching his features.

"Please? I need to tell you what I found."

His shoulders sag as he turns and sulks along behind me. I halt in the space between the cars where we have the rushing wind to hide our conversation and the advantage over anyone approaching.

"What's going on? Did Lulu remember something else?"

Oops. I forgot about the part where he doesn't know I went to search Mr. Elliott's compartment.

Maybe if I fast-forward past the breaking and entering, he'll stay focused on the more important discoveries.

"I know that look, Moon. What did you do?"

"I kind of searched Orson's room."

Erick throws his hands in the air. "You just won't be satisfied until you're dead."

My mouth hangs open for a second. "You know what, Sheriff Harper, if I thought for one minute your anger had anything to do with me disobeying orders, I might take offense."

His hands collapse to his sides before reaching out and gripping both of mine. "I'm concerned about your safety. I don't want anything irreversibly bad to happen. Can't you understand? You know it's not about obedience, it's about you staying alive."

Pulling my hands from his, and resisting the urge to break into a Bee Gees anthem, I circle my arms around his waist and squeeze. "I'd be equally devastated if anything happened to you. But guess what I found?"

He sighs and kisses me tenderly. "What did your snooping uncover?"

"Orson Elliot, if that is his real name, is certainly the owner of the trunk that held me prisoner. The musty smell of old wood was unmistakable. His room is filled with all manner of disguises, including a fortuneteller getup. And did you catch how surprised he was to see me strolling freely through the train?"

Erick rubs his nose against mine and ushers me into the next first-class sleeping car. "Glad you're safe."

"It's all because of you. I was trapped inside Orson's room, banging for Silas to let me through, when you showed up in the passageway. I thought you knew I was in there."

He rubs a hand across his brow and shakes his head. "I did not. Thank goodness luck was on our side." Turning me toward the opposite end of the car, he leans into the back of my neck and whispers hotly in my ear. "The sooner we solve this case, the sooner I have you all to myself."

My mouth goes dry and my heart gallops in my chest. "Then we better hustle over to 1B and question Mlle. Lenormand immediately. It can't be a coincidence one of Orson's costumes was a dead ringer for her con-artist getup."

Mlle. Lenormand's strawberry-blonde waves are pulled back with a wide champagne-colored headband, and the matching silk robe tied tightly at her waist reveals precisely what I suspected. She's a shapely young woman with no hint of a French accent.

"Come in. Come in. I knew you would get to me sooner or later."

She crumples onto her lower sleeping berth, which has not been put away for the day, and arranges herself in a pitiable pose.

"Did we wake you?"

Adjusting the pillow behind her head, she presses a hand to her chest. "I'm suffering from one of my recurring bouts of ennui. I should be up and about trying to solve the silly mystery game, but once things took a dark turn with Dame Joanna, playtime lost its punch."

Wow. She's going to be a handful. I'd let Erick take the lead, but I seriously dislike the way she looks at him. "Understood. We need to confirm your whereabouts this morning, after midnight. Mr. Usher claims you spent the night in his compartment."

Her outward control of emotions continues to impress, but my actual psychic skills reveal hidden concern.

"I did no such thing. Mr. Usher is a rude bore. I'd rather spend all evening talking about agriculture with the Josephs. If you receive my meaning?"

Any way you slice it, her *meaning* is insulting to the sweet Josephs. Whether or not she throws shade on the despicable Mr. Usher is of no concern to me. "One of you is certainly lying. Why don't we start with your real name? That might help lift the suspicion from you."

Her heavily lidded eyes open wide. "My proper name is Lita Toppan. With an 'I,' not two 'Es.'"

Between you and me, I feel like the "I" speech is something she added later in life to reinforce the slice of dramatic flair, which fuels her. "Miss Toppan, why are you on this train?"

Something dark and utterly taboo slinks through her aura before she can compose herself with a reply. "The railway hired me to play this character for the game. Apparently it's more fun for the passengers if there's someone with an air of authenticity."

I'll spare her my feedback on her authenticity as a psychic. "So they paid you to participate in the game?"

"Hardly. That Dame Joanna is an insufferable penny pincher. She offered free first-class passage as compensation, and I've been paying myself in champagne ever since."

"Sounds like you and Joanna Hecht weren't on the best of terms. Did you have cause to dislike her enough to kill her?"

Once again, a sinister vibe emanates from the reclining diva. "I have no feelings either way about the deceased. My agent booked this gig, and I decided a train ride would be nice this time of year.

Nothing more, nothing less. You'll have to seek the guilty party elsewhere."

As though we had rehearsed it, Erick picks up the baton and delivers the *coup de grâce*. "How are you acquainted with Mr. Elliott?"

It doesn't take a set of extrasensory perceptions to see the cracks forming in her clever shell. "Who? Mr. Edward, did you say?"

Erick steps toward her and lowers his voice. "Don't play games. Mr. Elliott has an exact replica of your fortune-telling costume in his compartment. Is he your wardrobe manager, your accomplice, archnemesis—?"

"Enough. Enough." She pushes herself up from her pillows and hugs her robe close to her bosom as one side slips off her shoulder. "Mr. Elliott is hardly what he seems."

Thankfully, Erick takes no notice of her blatant attempt to distract him. "Why don't you enlighten us?"

I have to grin as my guy crosses his arms and exhales.

She pulls out an onyx cigarette holder from under her pillow and holds it between her fingers as she speaks. In case you were wondering, there's no cigarette in it, and it never touches her lips. Apparently it's a prop.

"Mr. Elliott is none other than my sister Lizzie

in one of her many disguises. She's been jealous of my superior talents her entire life. Despite her over-the-top attempts, she has always been two steps behind. I'm the one in the limelight; she's always lurking in the shadows."

My mood ring tingles softly and replays the image of the circus. "Who joined the circus first? You or Lizzie?"

The former Mlle. Lenormand, now Lita Toppan, gasps and fixes me with eyes brimming with genuine shock. "Did you—? Who told—?"

"Answer the question."

"Lizzie joined first, but she came begging for help when things got ugly, and she found out how much more they'd pay for a sister act."

Little pieces fall into place, and I smile with satisfaction. "More than sisters. Twins."

She waves the cigarette holder as though she can erase the past. "Yes. Twins. So exhausting. Names that 'go together,' clothes that match, the same haircuts, the same classes . . . Like I said, exhausting."

And a moment later clarity grips me. "You were the one, weren't you?"

She shakes her head and dangles the cigarette holder impatiently. "The *one* what?"

"You were the one Joanna Hecht adopted. You, not your sister."

The vintage holder tumbles to the carpet with a soft thud. "Who told you?"

"When did you and your sister hatch this plan for revenge? Was it when Dame Joanna refused to save you from the orphanage, or more recently?"

The apprehension in her body is tangible. "There's no possible— Alice!"

Erick grips her small wrist in his large hand. "Let's go see if there's a pair of handcuffs we can borrow."

She struggles fruitlessly, and Erick's grip holds firm as she protests. "I'm innocent. I swear to you, I'm innocent. Lizzie is the one with the grudge, not me. I didn't even know she wrote that letter. She said it was from both of us, but I had no part in it. I found the cruel reply from Joanna Hecht after Lizzie vanished—*after* she ran away from that infernal home for the forgotten."

My curiosity has the better of me. "Where did she go after she left the orphanage?"

"The circus was passing through town and the holy sisters refused to take us to a spectacle that glorified the display of half-naked women. Lizzie thought it sounded glamorous and exotic. She escaped in the night. A few months later, she wrote to me from somewhere on the East Coast. The ringmaster was abusing her, and the hours were insufferable. Lizzie was always a follower, never a leader.

She needed me, so I went. I was a year away from getting booted out of the orphanage anyway. I came to her rescue, as always, and we had a decent career touring the world with our high-wire act."

"How did you end up this far north, with nothing but a crystal ball and a pack of tarot cards?" Erick releases his hold on her arm and waits for an answer.

She rubs her wrist as though it had been clamped in a bear trap. "You age out of the circus pretty quickly. I was always good at reading people. There's a lot of money to be made in telling fortunes."

Part of me still doesn't like the fraud, but the other part of me understands the need to do whatever it takes to survive. Been there. Done that. My days as a broke barista are not that far behind me.

The *mademoiselle* continues. "Before she ran away from the orphanage, Lizzie broke into the main office and stole my adoption records. When I confronted her, she claimed she wanted to find our birth mother, but I always suspected something darker. Lizzie tends toward the dramatic."

If Grams were here, I'm sure she'd ask the girl if she was the pot or the kettle in that scenario.

"Who booked you on this train?" Erick narrows his gaze.

"My sister Lizzie, of course. She takes care of

my arrangements, and she covers for me when I have my spells. That's why she has a copy of my fortune teller costume. As to the other nonsense in her compartment, I can't comment."

He leans toward her. "Did you or your sister have anything to do with Dame Joanna's death?"

The lifelong charlatan attempts a tear, but none fall. "I can assure you I had nothing to do with this. I moved on ages ago."

I step forward and clear my throat. "I notice you were careful not to mention your sister in your answer. Do you think Lizzie had something to do with Dame Joanna's murder?"

The diva's eyelids droop with disinterest. "We drifted apart. She handles my bookings through some online portal, and, if I'm lucky, I never have to see her. I wasn't sure she'd bother to ride the train, until I saw her skulking around that little mixer. I thought perhaps she was too good to work as my understudy. She fancies herself a publicist now. Apparently she's helping some farmer turn his business into an agricultural behemoth."

My hand immediately goes to Erick's arm, and I squeeze hard. To his credit, he doesn't jump. "Miss Toppan, I'm confining you to your compartment. I'll notify the porters and the train security. If you leave this compartment, I will arrest you for homicide. This is your last chance to cooperate."

She swoops forward and retrieves her cigarette holder. "I've told you everything I know, officer."

The muscles in his jaw tighten, but he nods and leads me out of her room.

"Let's head into the restaurant car and see if they can scare up a cup or two of liquid alert. The lack of sleep is finally catching up with me."

His head nods affirmatively, but he doesn't appear to be listening.

"Erick, are you thinking what I'm thinking?"

His head drags upward and eventually those intelligent eyes focus on me. "Almost never."

The deadpan reply catches me off guard. "Wait. What?" I brush his joke away with a flick of my wrist. "Agricultural behemoth? What if Lizzie Toppan is working for the Josephs?"

"What if she is? I suppose that does more to explain how they ended up on the train than anything else."

"Didn't Bernie say he farms apricots and cherries?" My head nods up and down, and I finally have Erick's full attention. "It would've been simple for her to get her hands on the raw materials to distill her own cyanide."

He accepts a cup of coffee that he didn't ask for and holds it in both hands as though he's cold. "Sorry, Moon. I'm sure you have a great point, but something just doesn't sit right with me about Lita's story."

"Which part?" I attempt a cheesy French accent. "The part where she's so amazing that all her sister can do is run around lapping at her heels, or the part where they mysteriously 'aged out' of the circus?"

He chuckles at my hijinks. "Sounds like I *was* thinking what you were thinking, but without the accent. I'm curious about both of those things, but I'm also wondering about the publicity angle. If this sister, Lizzie, fancies herself some kind of media mogul, maybe she had an accomplice."

"Margo Powell! I knew I didn't like that woman." Gulping down my coffee and pretending it doesn't burn prevents me from offering up my plan.

"I need to get Orson Elliott a.k.a. Lizzie Toppan into custody. You seem to have some rapport with Ms. Powell. Why don't you track her down and see if you can get to the bottom of her involvement in this fiasco-turned-homicide?"

"How long until the depot?"

He checks his phone. "An hour and a half."

"Copy that. Good luck, Sheriff." I hand my empty cup to the porter and turn to exit.

Erick catches me and pulls me into a tender embrace. "Be careful. And that's not an order, it's a heartfelt request."

Grinning like the Cheshire cat, I shrug. "I'm always careful."

He exhales with nearly as much drama as Mlle. Lenormand, and marches off to clap the irons on his suspect.

Before I head off to Margo Powell's compartment, a random thought pops into my head. Who is the biological mother of the terror twins?

Sliding that query to a back burner, I hear raised voices in the Josephs' double compartments. I knock lightly on 1A.

Tootie opens the door and, despite the raised voices, her face is drained of all color.

"What's going on? Are you all right?"

She shakes her head, ignores Bernie's shushing, and spills her news. "I think that Orson Elliott fella isn't a real person."

"What do you mean? I've seen him. He looks real." No need to spill the costume-loving-potential-murderer news.

She waves her flustered hands and gestures to Bernie. "You tell her. I'm not saying it right."

Bernie steps to the door and tilts his head toward me conspiratorially. "She thinks Mr. Elliott is our publicist in disguise. Now, don't go thinking she's crazy.

She's got an overactive imagination. It's one of the things I love about her, and the doctor tells us it keeps her young. But she's beside herself with this fantasy."

Placing my hand on Bernie's shoulder, I give it a squeeze. "I hate to be the one to break it to you, but Tootie is one hundred percent right this time. I mean, if your publicist is Lizzie Toppan."

Tootie presses both her hands to her face in shock. She looks exactly like the kid from *Home Alone*. "I knew it!"

Bernie shakes his head and exhales long and slow. "Boy, oh boy. I sure am sorry, honey. Not everyone has that eye for detail like you."

"So, Lizzie Toppan is your publicist?"

Bernie nods, and Tootie offers a stream of yep, yep, yeps.

"Can I ask you a weird question?"

Bernie shrugs. "Seems like the day for it."

"Did you ship her any sample product while she was working on your publicity campaign?"

Bernie rubs a hand across his mouth and nods in slow motion. "A heckuva lot, if I remember correctly. She kept telling me how important it was for her to believe in the product she was promoting."

"Well, thank you. I have a couple of things to follow up on, but I appreciate this additional information."

They both nod warmly as I leave, and I can't

help but linger for a moment as Bernie places an arm around Tootie's shoulders and offers another heartfelt apology. They are absolutely the sweetest. One day, maybe . . .

Next stop, Margo Powell.

Knock. Knock. Knock.

"Now what?" She's changed out of her loungewear, and into a flashy gown with a plunging neckline.

"Dressed for supper already?"

She scoffs. "I'm about mid-process. How can I help you, Mitzy?"

"I guess the best way would be if you can offer some explanation as to your relationship with Lizzie Toppan. And if it's not too much trouble, maybe you could tell me what the two of you had planned for Dame Joanna? Or was the murder what you had planned?"

Margo gasps and drops her ostentatious earring. "If that little minx is trying to throw me under the bus—"

"So when you told us Orson Elliott spent the night in your room, that was just another way of saying you and Lizzie were firming up your alibis?"

"Alibi? I don't need an alibi to write a story, honey. Lizzie promised me an exclusive. She claimed to have the goods on that 'Dame' Joanna blowhard. It's the kind of story that could get me national attention."

My eyes widen and I can't control my outrage. "You were so desperate for attention that you planned a murder? Just for the headline?"

Margo points one of her frighteningly long fingernails in my direction. "You may think I'm a has-been, but a journalist never forgets her training. I recorded every conversation I ever had with that Lizzie woman. Whether that double-crossing hussy knew about it or not! And you best believe me when I tell you, she never so much as whispered the word 'murder.'"

"Sheriff Harper is going to need those recordings."

"You're standing there, accusing me of first-degree murder. Do you really think I'm going to turn over the only thing I have that will guarantee me a plea deal?"

"It's starting to sound a lot like you knew what Lizzie was planning. And if you knew she was planning to kill a woman on this train and did nothing to stop her, I think that's pretty much the definition of *accomplice*."

Margo lunges toward the beaded handbag on her open berth, and my claircognizance screams the word "gun!"

Once again, I owe some thanks to foster brother

and schoolyard bully, Jarrell, for my training. My fist crashes into her face and my foot hits her square in the abdomen to shove her backward in the small space. She screams and clutches her face. "My nose! You broke my nose! A ten-thousand-dollar nose job down the drain. I ought to charge you with assault."

Opening the handbag, I tilt it toward her and display the small revolver. "I'm pretty sure the jury will see my side when I explain to them that an accomplice in a double-murder scheme attempted to silence me."

Blood is dripping down her fancy gown as I step into the hallway and shout for Bernie. Some people may look at him as over the hill, but I know the ilk of a man who can handle himself when I see one.

Mr. Josephs rushes out of his compartment. "Mitzy? What's going on?"

I tip the handbag toward him. "Ms. Powell is involved in the murder plot that took Joanna Hecht's life. And when I confronted her, she tried to shoot me."

He stomps forward with the fury of a mother bear. "You hand me that gun, little lady. I'll make sure she doesn't move a muscle until we hit the depot in Sault Ste. Marie."

"Thanks, Bernie. I thought you looked like the kinda guy who knew how to take care of business."

He nods, widens his stance, and trains the gun on Margo.

Tootie emerges, instantly takes in the scene, and smiles proudly. "I'll let the Who's Who know what's going on. You go tell your sheriff how Mitzy Moon got her woman." She chuckles at her own line, and I hurry back to Mlle. Lenormand's cabin to ask my burning question.

CHAPTER 14

Lita Toppan doesn't respond when I bang on
her cabin door. Since I'm not one to stand on ceremony, I let myself in. The previously weak and list-
less fortuneteller is hell-bent on forcing fate in her
favor. Her carpetbag is open on the berth, and she's
shoving clothing, jewels, and a canister of mace into
the satchel as fast as her hands can go.

"Excuse me, Lita."

She screams and spins on the heels of her
winter boots. "What are you doing here? Who let
you in?"

"I believe Sheriff Harper confined you to your
compartment. You seem to be packing in quite a
hurry. Going somewhere?"

She grumbles under her breath. "I'm not sure if
you and your backwoods lawman have figured it out

yet, but my unhinged sister is setting me up to take the fall for this!"

"If you're innocent, you have no reason to run. We know both victims were poisoned, and we have every reason to believe that your sister manufactured the poison herself. A search of her residence should provide the missing pieces of evidence the prosecution will need to put her away. However, I tend to agree. She tried to throw suspicion on you. Can you tell me why?"

Lita throws the canister of mace into her bag and sighs. "I already told you. Lizzie has always been in my shadow. Apparently she decided it was her time to shine. She must have assumed that if she could get me out of the way, she could finally *become* me."

"As an only child who spent almost half my childhood in foster care, I don't know a whole lot about sisters. Assuming Lizzie has this lifelong jealousy you keep mentioning, and possibly an unhealthy dash of homegrown sociopathic tendencies, you could be right. But running away isn't going to prove you're innocent."

She waves her hands wildly. "What about Lizzie? Why aren't you confining her to her quarters?"

"Erick—Sheriff Harper—is taking care of that.

The only reason I came back was to ask you a question."

She rolls her eyes. "Ask away. I have no more secrets."

"You mentioned Lizzie stole your adoption records when she escaped from the orphanage. When you went after her and joined the circus, you must've had a chance to look at them. Didn't you ever try to find your birth mother?"

Lita brushes her hair from her eyes, tilts her head, and glances out the window. "It was a dead end. The scared young woman probably provided a false name when she gave us up. We could never find any trace of her."

"So you dropped the search? All the advances in technology and the new websites available to adopted children—"

"Yes, I decided it was best to let sleeping dogs lie. I can't speak for Lizzie. She tends toward —disturbed."

"What was the name on the adoption papers?"

She presses a hand to her arched eyebrow and bites her lip. "Oh my. It was years ago. Let me think . . . The last name was Lucas. The first name started with an M, or was it an N. No, definitely an M . . . Marilu. There! You've mined me for all that I have."

"Thank you, Lita. I'm sorry things have gone so

wrong with your sister. I'm not gonna stop you from whatever it is you're doing, but, if you run, you'll never truly be free."

And with that platitude, I leave her compartment and close the door. I wonder how hard they looked for Marilu? *If* Lita is being honest with me, and my extra senses didn't pick up on any falsehood, she genuinely doesn't care one way or the other. Lizzie, on the other hand, may have kept searching for Marilu Lucas.

Wait! Marilu Lucas? Lulu? It can't be! Rushing down the passageway and through the doors between the cars, I hurry to my own room.

Lulu is resting comfortably, and Silas is preparing chamomile tea. "Good afternoon, Mitzy. What have you and the sheriff uncovered?"

Jerking my thumb toward the patient, I ask, "Can I talk to her?"

Silas nods, and his jowls bounce up and down. "Indeed. She has recovered her full mental faculties, and a good deal of her physical strength. I'm preparing a spot of tea to coax her a few steps farther toward recovery."

"Copy that." I gently take a seat next to Lulu as I press my hands across my thighs toward my knees.

The names, Marilu Lucas and Lulu Weathers, could be pure coincidence. If I go down this road, there's no turning back. If I'm wrong, the false accusation could cause a tiny upset to her recovery. And if I'm right— That probably goes double. "Lulu, I need to ask you something, and it's incredibly personal. I'm going to apologize in advance, but it could be very important to the investigation."

She reaches a shaky hand toward me and pats my knee. "After today's events, dear, I think I'm prepared for almost anything. Especially if it will help the investigation. I can't imagine who did this to me."

I sincerely hope I can spin this toward the happy news end of the dial. "Lulu, were you ever known by another name?"

Her mouth answers no, but her head nods in the affirmative. That outward juxtaposition is not the only indication of conflict. "Are you sure? Does the name Marilu Lucas mean anything to you?"

The faint color that had returned to her cheeks drains instantly. Her body becomes rigid and her fingers curl into fists.

The predominant vibe wafting toward me is abject fear.

"No one outside this room has to know. I don't want to cause you any difficulty. But if you were Marilu Lucas, and you gave up twin girls for adoption, I have some news."

She avoids eye contact and extends her hand toward the tea tray.

"Silas, is the tea ready?"

When I reach for the cup, he slips his finger into the liquid and traces the commanding truth symbols. I remember his somber mood when he taught them to me, and his warning speech, as though it were yesterday: *This is no parlor trick. This is a powerful transmutation, and you should know better than most how truth can be a double-edged sword. It is not a skill to be abused. It is a potent tool, to be wielded with the precision of a scalpel.* If he's choosing to use this tool now, he shares my urgent need for facts.

His milky blue eyes connect with mine and I see the sparks. "It is." He passes me the saucer and cup, and I offer them to Lulu.

She sips the tea as she gazes out the window. There's something about the angle of her nose and the tilt of her chin that calls to mind a similar gaze from Lita.

After she's taken several sips of the tea, and I'm certain the symbols have done their work to loosen her tongue, I reopen my line of questioning. "Lulu, did you give up two twin girls for adoption?"

Her thin lips press together, but the alchemical transmutation of the liquid overpowers. "Yes." Lulu's head turns and her eyes widen in horror.

I attempt a reassuring smile. "Don't worry, your secret is safe with us. All those years ago, were you aware that Dame Joanna was the one who was adopting your girls?"

She shakes her head and exclaims, "What? The woman who was killed? Oh dear." Lulu bows her head and whispers a silent prayer before responding to my question. "My parents were very religious, very strict. Such an indiscretion would've brought so much shame to the family. My father was a minister, my mother played the organ at the church—it was a disaster. They sent me to live with my aunt, and she and my mother organized everything. I had no idea what happened to the girls. No way to find them . . ."

I place a comforting hand on her shoulder. "You're not to blame. You were a child yourself, and they made decisions for you that you might not have made if you'd had control. I have some good news and some bad news." Exhaling, I look at the floor. "I'll be honest with you—it's mostly bad news."

Her hand reaches toward my knee again. "Tell me. I'm ready. I spent the last thirty-five years regretting my decision. I may as well learn the truth."

"How about I start with the bad news, and we work our way toward the silver lining?"

Gentle tears trickle down her face as she nods.

It's a struggle to keep judgment from my voice,

but I'm not here to speak ill of the dead. "Dame Joanna refused to adopt both babies. She only adopted the one that became known as Lita Toppan. The other girl, Lizzie, remained at the orphanage. However, Dame Joanna's husband died unexpectedly about a year after the adoption, and she had a breakdown. No longer able to take care of the girl, she returned Lita to the orphanage just before her sixth birthday. Roughly a decade later, after both girls had been passed over for adoption several times, Lizzie, the one who had been left behind all along, wrote a letter to Dame Joanna, offering their slave labor in exchange for the rescue of her and her sister from the orphanage."

Lulu grips my hand and squeezes. "Did she take them?"

"Sadly, no. By all accounts, she was an austere woman who wasn't influenced by the plight of two young girls. Shortly after the curt refusal, Lizzie ran away from the facility. She joined the circus, was treated poorly, and wrote for her sister to save her."

The broken woman next to me on the bench cries softly. "So much sadness. I caused such harm."

"I don't think you should blame yourself. I'm pretty sure a psychological evaluation will clearly expose Lizzie's underlying mental instabilities."

Lulu sniffles, and Silas hands her his handkerchief.

She dabs at her eyes. "What does all this have to do with the train and Dame Joanna's death?"

"Sheriff Harper's currently placing Lizzie Toppan under arrest for the murder of Dame Joanna, and I'm pretty sure she'll also be charged with your attempted murder."

Lulu gasps and leans back in the seat. "Oh, dear! What have I done?"

"Once again, you've done nothing. There is some good news, I think. I saved the best bit for last."

She shakes her head and draws a ragged breath. "I'm not sure I deserve good news. I made such horrible choices. One youthful indiscretion has ruined so many lives."

"There's a chance for redemption."

She tilts her head toward me. "Tell me."

"The other girl, Lita Toppan, is the woman who played Mlle. Lenormand in our mystery game. She's upset about her sister, and of course has her own emotional baggage. Don't we all. But I think I could facilitate a meeting, if you'd like?"

Lulu drops the handkerchief in her lap and grips my hand with both of hers. "I would. Oh, I would so much like to meet her, Mitzy. I'll do what I can for Lizzie, and if there's a chance I could salvage a real relationship with just one of them, it would change my life." She presses a hand to her mouth and shakes her head. "Thank the Lord I don't have to tell my husband, God rest him. But I'll need to explain all this to my son, and a condensed version to my congregation . . . I suppose if I don't take this opportunity to confess my sins, I can never truly embrace His forgiveness."

I'm not nearly as familiar with the ins and outs of religious doctrine as Pastor Weathers, but I'll take her word for it. "I'll go and have a chat with—"

Thundering footsteps crash against the metal shell above us. My head whips to Silas as my inner knowing delivers the news I least want to know. "Erick is on top of the train!"

Silas nods as though I've told him it was raining. "Perhaps he's in need of assistance."

Bolting from the compartment, I race to the end of the sleeping car, open the door, and step into the "in between." The track is racing by beneath me as I place an unsteady hand on the small iron ladder leading up.

Oh, to be a svelte and coordinated girl. I pull myself up the ladder, one heart-pounding step at a time, and my knuckles clutch the metal rungs in a death grip.

When my head pops above the rim of the train car, the force of the wind is immense.

Petite Lizzie Toppan is galloping across the top of the train car like a monkey through the treetops.

She leaps from one car to the next with stunning aerobatic grace.

The only reason Erick can keep up is strength, coordination, and a long stride.

There's nothing I can do. There's no way I can run across a moving train car. The best thing I can do is get to the engineer, from inside the train cars, and stop this thing.

Hang on, Erick! Help is on its way. It's taking a roundabout path, but I promise it's coming.

CHAPTER 15

THERE LITERALLY COULD NOT BE MORE people in my way as I race toward the front of the train. Every sleeping car is littered with porters, the restaurant car seems to be serving an irresistible round of pre-supper appetizers, and everyone in the coach-class passenger cars simultaneously needs items from their carry-on at this exact moment.

The smell of fuel is thick in the air when I finally reach the tank locomotive. I discover its modern addition of a security door and—it's locked. Without giving a great deal of thought to my approach, I bang wildly and shout incoherent pleas for help through the thick glass.

The engineer shakes his head in the negative, and points for me to return from whence I came.

I shake my head right back and continue to pound on the door.

He picks up an old-fashioned CB radio microphone, and a voice blasts out of the speaker above my head. "Return to your compartment, Miss. No one is allowed in the cab but the engineer, the fireman, and the conductor."

I'm not sure if the speaker is one-way or two-way, but it's worth a shot. "Sheriff Harper is in trouble!"

"Miss, if you don't return to your compartment immediately, I will call security."

Perfect. That's exactly what I want. I dig out my tension wrench and lock pick, and go to work.

He continues to threaten me over the loudspeaker, but I'm too busy picking the lock to notice if he's making good on any of those threats.

Click, spin, and the door opens.

I smile triumphantly.

He pulls a gun.

Plot twist! My hands go up instantly. "Don't shoot! Sheriff Harper is in trouble! That's what I've been trying to tell you. He knows who the murderer is, and he's chasing her across the top of the train!"

The engineer tilts his head and his face looks like it wants to believe me.

Thankfully, I have a few extra senses that confirm what his face is saying. "Please, put the gun down. You have to stop the train."

"And how do I know you're not the murderer setting up this whole dirty trick just so I'll pull the brake and give you an opportunity to escape?"

I lift my hands higher in the air and nod. "That's a great question. You *don't* know that. The only thing I can tell you is that my name is Mitzy Moon. My dad, Jacob Duncan, owns the Midwest Union Railway, and—"

"Hold on now! You're tellin' me you're ol' Cal Duncan's granddaughter?"

"Please, stop the train. We can discuss all of this later."

He turns to the man on his left, who remained oddly silent during our heated exchange. "Call security and tell 'em to head to the caboose on the double."

Lowering my hands, I offer a smile. "Thank you. I'll go see if I can help your guy in the caboose."

As I turn, I realize how that phrase sounds out loud. No time for wordsmithing. I need to hightail it.

The fates smile down on my return trip, and the folks in the aisles and passageways seem to part like the Red Sea.

The scrape of brake shoes on metal wheels reassures me that the engineer believes my story.

When I pass by Margo Powell's compartment, I convince Bernie to give me the gun.

"You sure you know how to handle that, Mitzy?"

"Just like shootin' tuna off the paddle cactus back in Boynton Canyon."

He hands me the gun and chuckles. "What do I do if this one makes a run for it?"

I wink at Tootie and squeeze his bicep. "A big guy like you oughta be able to keep things under control."

He blushes and Tootie giggles. "We'll handle it. You get goin'!"

By the time I make it to the caboose, there's an acrid odor of hot metal rising up from the tracks and the train has slowed considerably. I probably slept through far more physics classes than I should have, so I don't know the calculation for mass, velocity, and bringing it all to a halt, but I know it takes a long time to stop a train.

The brakes are screeching loudly now and smoke rises from the steel wheels.

The passengers in the caboose are being herded out like misbehaving cattle.

"No time to explain. I need you all to exit the viewing car immediately." The gruff security officer is waving, and possibly doing a bit of shoving, and the confused passengers offer their protests.

"We paid extra to sit here."

"I'm not sure it's appropriate for you to ask us to leave."

"Why is the train stopping?"

And of course the classic, "I'm going to speak to the owner."

Good luck on that last one, buddy. Unless you're some kind of clairvoyant medium, you're not going to be getting an audience with Dame Joanna anytime soon.

Stepping onto the viewing platform at the back of the caboose, I promptly ignore all Erick's warnings.

Taking more risk than he would approve, I step over the railing of the viewing platform, grip the narrow ladder on the side of the caboose, and hope my weapon doesn't fall as I climb. The gun is tucked firmly in the back of my waistband, but my larger concern is being able to aim when my hand will surely be shaking from anxiety and cold.

As I peek above the edge of the railcar, Erick and Lizzie are in a standoff. She seems to be using her own life as a bargaining chip and threatening to jump from the train.

When I glance up the tracks, my face becomes a

cartoon expression. The train is heading into a tunnel. Of all the movie tropes to hold true at this point in time, I can't believe it's going to be a tunnel.

As the train slides closer to the opening in the basalt rock, it's still carrying significant velocity.

Lizzie screams.

Upon examination, I don't blame her. The opening appears to be shrinking in size as we approach. I have a sneaking suspicion that this tunnel's vertical height maximums will not accommodate people running on the top of train cars.

Erick, as usual, is pulling out all the stops to preserve human life. He looks over his shoulder at the looming tunnel, but inches closer to Lizzie.

Her desperation triples.

Glancing at the approaching tunnel, I pretend to calculate how long I have before I'm scraped off the side of the train by a brick arch. I'd have to say two minutes—max.

Erick is a mere ten feet from Lizzie.

She reaches into the pocket of her coat and pulls a gun.

Now there's something I wasn't expecting from a dedicated poisoner!

Sheriff Harper puts up his hands, and, although I can see the movement of his lips, it's my extrasensory perception that hears his words above the screech of the train.

"Put the gun down, Lizzie. Throw it. You don't want to hurt any more people."

My psychic gifts take over and I hear every word as though I'm seated between them on that tin roof.

Her low, calculating laughter gives me a worse case of gooseflesh than the frigid wind. "I killed my own mother to keep her quiet, Sheriff. What in the world makes you think I would hesitate to pull this trigger on you?"

"Lulu is still alive, Lizzie. You have a chance to make things right with her." He takes another step.

Rather than relief, Lizzie exudes a dark rage. "Impossible. I've been studying the effects of cyanide for nearly two years. Every piece of this puzzle was so carefully plotted—"

Time to make an executive decision. We do not have time for this. I hook one elbow through the ladder and pull the gun out of my waistband. Using the roof of the car as a brace, I aim and shoot.

She screams and falls toward the center of the car.

Erick's head snaps toward the gunshot's point of origin. His expression carries gratitude mixed with panic.

"Mitzy! Get down from there. Now!"

The tunnel is mesmerizingly close. Fear is forcing my hands to grip the bars too tightly.

He kicks Lizzie's gun from the train, scoops her under one arm, and runs at me in a low crouch. His eyes bore into my heart. "Down. Now."

And suddenly I'm a soldier on a battlefield. I follow the instructions of my commanding officer without question. Backing down the ladder at record speed, I swing a leg over the railing and land on the viewing platform—alone—just as the train plunges into the tunnel.

My scream echoes off the stone and tears sluice down my cheeks.

The blackness is suffocating.

There's no light at the end of the tunnel.

There is no light in my world.

CHAPTER 16

IT DOESN'T TAKE LONG for my internal "Debbie Downer" to take over. Ever since my unfortunate babysitter had to deliver the news of my mother's tragic death, I've been waiting for the other shoe to drop.

Consider this a resounding thud.

With my knees pulled firmly to my chest, my head bowed, and sobs racking my body, I have to admit, this seems like the end of the line.

I knew things were going too well for Mitzy Moon. I was feeling happy, satisfied, and, dare I say it, proud of myself.

My shoulders are shaking and the tearstain on my jeans has soaked through to the skin.

Guess who's the new poster child for "pride cometh before the fall?" And what a spectacular fall it was. I wish I could go back in time and prevent the ripples of my cursed fate from hitting Erick.

Handsome, good-hearted, kind, selfless—

"Mitzy? Mitzy, are you crying?"

My head pops up and I search the caboose platform.

We're out of the tunnel, for what it's worth. However, there's absolutely no one but me in this viewing area.

Oh my gosh! Not only did I manage to get Erick Harper killed, but now his ghost is haunting me.

"I'm so sorry, Erick. I never should've gotten you involved in this. Now you're dead, and it's all my fault. You have every right to haunt me."

His relieved laughter echoes off the hard surfaces. "I'm not laughing at you, Moon. I'm laughing with you."

Jumping to my feet, I stomp indignantly. "I'm not laughing! This is no laughing matter, Erick Harper. I'm responsible for your death."

The limp, whimpering body of Lizzie Toppan tumbles over the railing. Gasping, I step back, but can't tear my eyes away from the blood.

"Wait. How did she—?"

And that's when the best-looking tactical boot I've ever seen steps onto the railing.

Erick ducks his head as he jumps onto the platform.

Dead bodies and decorum can kiss my— I lunge forward and squeeze him tighter than any child has ever squeezed a plushy on a carnival midway.

"So you thought I was dead, eh?"

My hands grab his face and pull it toward me. Without even taking the time to wipe my tears, I kiss him so hard I can't breathe.

He hugs me tightly and whispers, "Easy, Moon. Save some of this initiative for the trip home."

For the first time since the train disappeared into the darkness, my heart feels light. "Everything was going too good. I thought my luck had finally taken a deadly turn."

He places his finger under my chin and tips my puffy, tear-stained face toward his gorgeous stubbled chin. "It's not luck. It's when preparation meets opportunity."

"Oh brother!"

Pulling me to the side with one arm, he gestures toward the simpering sociopath. "What are we gonna do with her?"

"I only winged her, on the leg. I say we pour a bottle of vodka on it and let her tough it out until Sault Ste. Marie."

He nods. "Sounds fair."

Finally, feeling enough calm to regain a shred of

vanity, I wipe away my tears and take a deep breath.

He bends and grips Lizzie firmly by the arm. "Lizzie Toppan, I'm placing you under arrest for the murder of Dame Joanna Hecht and the attempted murder of Lulu Weathers. Is there anything I missed?"

At first, she shakes her head, but quickly changes tactics. "You may as well know that Margo Powell was working with me this whole time."

Erick looks over his shoulder at me and raises his eyebrows.

I smile, nod, and shoot down Lizzie's bravado. "Yeah, Lizzie, I already figured that out. Margo is under house arrest in her compartment. And she threw you under the bus pretty eagerly. No honor among murdering schemers, I guess."

He pushes Lizzie forward, and she plays off an exaggerated limp as she continues to cast dispersions on Margo. "This whole thing was mostly her idea. She thought a good scandal would get her career back on track. She thinks she's some kind of Barbara Walters."

Erick steers her through the baggage car. "Was it her idea to put Mitzy in a trunk?"

She turns and offers a smug grin. "Not at all. That's what I like to call an 'ad lib.'"

Stepping forward, I narrow my gaze and lift my

chin. "Then I'd like to say, I'm not sorry I shot you, Lizzie. Maybe I should fire off a round at your other leg. You smug little—"

He gestures for me to simmer down.

Lizzie pants dramatically and immediately leaps onto the new topic. "I'm going to sue you for attempted murder! Not so smart now, are you?"

I click my tongue in mockery, but before I can launch my snark assault, Erick jumps to my defense.

"You were threatening an officer of the law with a loaded weapon. Mitzy was well within her rights to offer me protection."

Lizzie chuckles. "Good luck proving that, Sheriff. You kicked my gun off the train."

The triumphant chuckle that escapes from Sheriff Harper surprises me. "I happen to know one of the K-9 officers in Sault Ste. Marie personally. She's got a heckuva reputation for weapons recovery. I have full faith in her ability to find that missing firearm."

Suddenly, I'm all ears. Who is this "she" in Sault Ste. Marie? He's never mentioned it to me before. I realize he's talking about a dog, but I'm still pretty jealous. I mean, K-9 officers don't work alone. This amazing dog's partner better be a guy.

When my focus returns to the events at hand, Erick has paused to accept a pair of handcuffs from the security officer. But before he locks them around Lizzie's wrists, he looks at me and winks playfully. And, as though he's been reading my mind, he offers me some comfort. "Don't worry, she's not my type."

"Rude."

His crooked grin teases me. "I'm going to collect Margo. Then the security officer and I will guard the prisoners until we reach our destination. Why don't you head back to the compartment and check on Lulu?"

Right, he doesn't know about the whole Marilu Lucas angle. Plenty of time to catch him up as we ride the rails back to Pin Cherry.

When I reach my compartment, I hear animated voices coming from inside, and open the door slowly.

"Am I interrupting?"

Silas smiles and gestures for me to take a place on the bench seat beside him. As soon as I drop onto the soft, cushioned seat, the emotional exhaustion hits me like a freight train. Sorry, it was unintentional. It was either a freight train or a Mack truck, and after the day I've had, I think freight train fits the bill.

Lita Toppan a.k.a. Mlle. Lenormand offers me a kind smile. "You were right, Mitzy. Running away wasn't the answer. I correctly assumed that if

Lizzie attacked Lulu, then there must be a connection."

Lulu smiles. "I've told Lita as much as I know. Thank you for this moment, Mitzy."

"You're welcome. You're both welcome. I'm glad you chose to stay, Lita."

She sighs. "I hate to ask: Did you catch my sister?"

"Absolutely. I shot her myself."

The women gasp, and Silas turns a stern glare in my direction.

"She and Erick were on top of the train, and she was threatening him with a gun. I only shot her in the leg. It's a through and through. She'll still be able to stand trial and enjoy many years in prison."

Lita hugs her arms around her waist. "I don't think there's anything anyone could have done for her. There was always something off. Even when we were quite small. I'm sure that's what Dame Joanna sensed about her, whether she knew it or not, at the orphanage."

Yeesh! Leave it to Mlle. Lenormand to find a way to compliment herself on the heels of her sister's arrest. "How are you feeling, Lulu?"

"I feel about as good as new. It honestly seems impossible to imagine that I was knocking at death's door earlier this very day."

Silas harrumphs. "Once again, you owe a debt of gratitude to Sheriff Harper."

"I do. Indeed, I do. And I also owe something to you, Mitzy. Your bravery and encouraging words helped me start the process of coming to terms with my secret past." She reaches out to take Lita's hand. "I've missed so very much of my daughter's life. There's no way I can make up for the lost birthdays or once-in-a-lifetime events, but moving forward . . . I hope you'll consider allowing me to be part of your life."

Lita swallows and her gaze drifts out the window.

I've been where she is. It might not have been thirty-plus years, but I was twenty-one when I came face-to-face with the ex-convict father I had assumed dead. "Speaking from experience, Lita, life is about choices. I grew up thinking I didn't have a father, and when I had the choice to let him in and see where it might lead, I could've shut it all down. That would've been a terrible mistake. There have been difficult times, and regrets, but now I have a family that's perfect for me." I tilt my head and smile. "Try not to have too many expectations. If you choose to allow Lulu into your life, just let it unfold."

Lita nods and squeezes her birth mother's hand. "It's a lot to take in. I'm sure you were in a terrible situation, with no control over your future. Right now, that doesn't make it any easier for me to understand why Lizzie and I had to suffer, but I appreciate the frame of reference."

Lulu nods and blinks back tears. "There's no pressure, sweetie. Thanks to Sheriff Harper's quick thinking, we both have many years ahead of us."

Lita nods and falls forward with a groan. She slumps onto the floor of the compartment and I stare in shock.

Silas looks at me. "Do you have the vial?"

"Maybe." I search in my front pocket and thankfully recover the amber vial—unbroken.

He points to Lita's crumpled form. "Tilt her head and pour the liquid in. Hopefully she retains enough consciousness to swallow."

I fall to my knees on the thick carpet and scoop her head onto my lap. Unscrewing the cap, I let it fall to the floor as I carefully dribble the greenish liquid into Lita's mouth.

Lulu breathes erratically. "What happened to her? What's going on?"

Silas calmly strokes his mustache with thumb and forefinger. "I fear Lizzie wasn't satisfied that her plan to incriminate Lita would be successful. It appears she has been slowly poisoning her sister to ensure that she would avail herself of the opportunity to take Lita's place one way or another."

Tears trickle down Lulu's face. "I've only just found her. I can't lose her now. Is it fatal? Is it cyanide like Lizzie gave me?"

Silas shakes his head. "This appears to be arsenic. Smaller doses repeated over a longer period of time." He directs his next question to me. "Were there no earlier symptoms?"

"She mentioned something about suffering bouts of ennui, but I thought it was all part of her overly dramatic shtick."

He exhales loudly. "It would appear not."

Lita blinks, gasps for air, and turns toward me in confusion. "What happened? Why am I on the floor?"

Silas and I bring her up to speed on the additional details of her sister's despicable back-up plan.

"She loves no one but herself."

Silas exhales loudly. "These are not the actions of an individual who loves herself. These are the actions of an individual who fears her very reflection."

A heavy silence hangs in the compartment as the train slowly chugs forward to complete its journey of revelations.

CHAPTER 17

WHEN, AT LAST, we pull into the depot in Sault Ste. Marie, over fifteen local police officers surge toward the train. The wave of blue covers every exit. Silas and I choose to sit tight while all the drama unfolds.

"Hold on a minute! I have Margo Powell's gun. I better turn this over and make sure it gets logged into evidence."

Before the door closes behind me, my wizened mentor offers an additional tip. "I'm sure you'll have to answer a few questions with regard to discharging the firearm as well."

"Copy that."

The view outside the windows of the train is surreal. Erick's blond bangs hang loosely as the magic-hour lighting bounces off his shoulders. The folks waiting on the platform step back in seeming awe when he guides the suspects forward with a firm hand on each.

A broad-shouldered woman, her black hair in a tight bun, walks toward him with a warm smile softening her imposing features. Her left hand holds the leash of a magnificent canine specimen. A muscular German shepherd with sharp ears and confident eyes trots gracefully at her side.

When I reach the door of the compartment, an overzealous police officer instructs me to return to my compartment.

"I'm with Sheriff Harper. I have information that's pertinent to the murder."

"I'm sorry, ma'am. We've been asked to keep all passengers on board."

Ma'am? He can't be serious. I know I'm going to regret this next part, but hopefully not for long. "I have a gun. And I shot—"

Before I can finish that sentence, I'm slammed against the steel train car, and the gun is yanked from my waistband. The odor of oil and solvent fills my nostrils as my face squishes against the newly painted railcar.

The officer slaps me in cuffs and shoves me, with a little more force than I feel is necessary, in front of him. I mean, I mentioned a gun, but it's not like I brandished it.

As we approach the "serve and protect" tête-à-tête, the commanding woman addresses Erick. "What's the deal with this third suspect, Harper? The guy on the squawk box said there were two." She places her hand on her gun and lifts her chin in my direction. Shades of Deputy Paulsen back in Pin Cherry Harbor flash through my head.

Without so much as turning his head, my wiseacre boyfriend addresses the woman in charge. "That would be Mitzy Moon, Lieutenant Juárez. She played an integral part in the capture of the two suspects. In fact, she's the one who shot Lizzie Toppan. Saved my life."

Lieutenant Juárez narrows her gaze and tosses a dangerous glare at the officer holding my arm. "Take the cuffs off her, McMillan."

Her authority is unquestioned. He immediately removes the cuffs and holds the confiscated gun in her direction.

"Drop it in an evidence bag. Gee whiz! This your first day on the job?"

He mumbles something close to an apology as he slinks away from the exchange.

Finally, Erick turns toward me and reveals his bemused smile. "How did you manage to get yourself—? Never mind. I'm not sure I even want to know."

Coming to my own defense, I offer my excuse. "I thought you might need the gun."

A tremor of brief laughter passes across his shoulders. "Lieutenant Juárez, let me introduce my girlfriend, Mitzy Moon. She identified the poison and figured out the connection between the accused murderer and Ms. Powell."

Margo mumbles something in her defense, but no one cares.

Lieutenant Juárez removes her hand from the gun and reaches toward me.

I grip her meaty paw and cringe internally, hoping she's not one of those bone crushing—spoke too soon. I bite my tongue and nod through the pain.

"Good to meet you, Moon. You did great work here. Anybody who's got Harper's back is good by me. Ever think of joining?"

My eyes widen and I stifle a snicker. "I do my best work in civilian clothes."

No one argues the point.

Gesturing to the magnificent animal, I ask, "Is this the dog you were talking about, Erick?"

The momentary bout of friendliness disappears, and Lieutenant Juárez once again places hand on gun. "This here's a K-9 officer. We don't call 'em dogs. It's beneath them. Harper tells me we've got a gun to recover from the tracks, less than a klick the other side of Baraga's tunnel, and Pookie here's gonna handle that."

Did she just say Pookie? I'm the bad guy because I called the K-9 officer a dog, but it's perfectly all right to name it something like Pookie! "Thanks, Lieutenant, that sounds great."

She nods to a couple of officers and they immediately step forward and accept the prisoners from Erick. "Thanks again, Harper. We'll take it from here. You and Ms. Moon can return to the train. My officers will be taking statements and releasing passengers to disembark. They'll move as quickly as they can. But you may want to notify your transportation of a two- to three-hour delay."

Erick nods. "10-4. We're booked on the return trip. And you can clear Silas Willoughby. He's with us. But I'll let the conductor know to pass the word among the porters. Can they continue with the food service?"

She nods. "Of course. Good to see you, Harper. We still on for that fishing trip in June?"

He laughs. "As long as you don't weasel out of the bet again. Biggest pike buys the beer. No exceptions."

She shakes her head and rubs a thumb along her bottom lip. "You better decide whether you mean by length or weight. Winners have to be specific, Harper. See ya 'round."

The lieutenant heads off the platform with her canine partner, and Erick slips an arm around my waist. "Did you wave the gun at the guy, or just threatened to?"

"Neither. I simply informed him I had a firearm."

He shakes his head. "Of course you did." He squeezes me and smiles. "Aren't you going to ask about my history with her, or the fishing trip?"

"Nope. I trust you."

Erick makes a comical screeching sound as he comes to an abrupt halt on the platform. "I'm not one to look a gift horse in the mouth, but I'm— You know what? Maturity looks good on you, Moon."

I'll take the compliment and not complain about being compared to a horse. Let him think it's all due to my fabulous maturity. He doesn't need to know that my psychic senses gave me a few hints about Juárez's prior military background. If she's one of the lucky ones in Erick's unit, then I'm not going to begrudge him a fishing trip. Although, now that I think about it—

He gently touches my face. "Seems like you drifted off for a minute? Everything okay?"

"What? Oh, sure. Yeah. Totally fine." My smile is pretty low-wattage, but I hope it's convincing.

"Well, we better get dressed for supper. I didn't pack a tuxedo for no reason."

My tummy tingles and flip-flops. "You're still planning on dressing for dinner?"

His head brushes against mine. "Unless you were planning on *undressing*."

Holy jelly knees, Batman! "We should definitely put on our fancy stuff. And I better check in with Grams. I'm sure she's worried sick."

"It's still strange to hear you talk about your deceased grandmother in the present tense, but it means a lot that you finally told me the truth."

"Yeah. It means a lot to me too." As we approach our train car, I stutter step to a halt. "Hold on. How are you alive right now?"

He turns to gaze down at me and scrunches up his face. "I'm sorry, did you want me to be dead?"

"That's not what I mean. You were on top of the train, and the tunnel wasn't big enough, and then you survived."

"Oh, that. The roof over the viewing platform on the back of the old caboose is about six inches lower than the main curve of the train car. Once you were safely on the platform, I pushed Lizzie onto that roof, flattened myself down beside her, and held her head down in case she got any crazy ideas. Once we cleared the tunnel, I tossed her down to the platform. Does that answer your question?"

"You're super smart, Erick Harper. That's what I like about you."

Pulling me closer, he whispers, "So you only like me for my brains?"

A huge bubble of emotion wells up in my gut. It feels like I'm ready. I think I'm going to say it out loud. If I don't faint first. "I like you for a lot of reasons. But, I love you for all of them."

Cut to—

Embarrassingly long, passionate kiss on the train depot platform as the sun sets behind us.

Fade to black.

All right, it probably won't set for another hour, but the film-school dropout in me couldn't resist setting the scene. And let me assure you, when I tell the story, and I will tell the story, it will be with the setting-sun detail.

Silas prepares to disembark with his official clearance, and Erick helps Lulu back to her compartment while I get changed.

The dress that Grams insisted I pack is more flattering than it looked on the hanger. The sleek black lines of the one-shoulder gown and the accent of silver Swarovski crystals swirling from just above the waist to the top of my thigh show off my figure perfectly.

A quick glance in the mirror confirms that something must be done about my hair. The only grown-up hairdo I've learned is a French roll. I'm not sure if that was a thing in the 1920s, but it's going to be a thing tonight.

I brush, backcomb, smooth, and twist. A small family of bobby pins must be sacrificed for this "do," but when all is said and done, I think Grams would be pleased.

As I pull my silver-toed black sling-backs from the closet, there's a soft knock at the door.

"Are you decent?"

"Almost never, but you can come in."

The door opens and, when Erick's eager face pops in, his shoulders droop for a moment when he sees that I'm dressed. "I think they call that false advertising, Moon."

I slip on my heels and do a pretty-princess spin in my dress. "You don't like?"

He glides his hands along my hips and grins. "You're a knockout."

A healthy blush rushes to my cheeks. "I'm going out to the passageway to call Grams while you get changed."

He shrugs and shakes his head. "Your loss."

Quickly stepping outside the compartment, I close the door and struggle to breathe. At this rate we'll never make it to supper, and a girl's gotta eat. Placing my call, I eagerly wait for Pye to answer.

The sight of a giant golden eye on my phone

sends a momentary spike of fright up my spine. "Move back, son. It's like I'm inside your head."

"Ree-ooooow." Concern.

"Mitzy? Is that finally you? We've been calling and calling! Is everything okay?"

"It is now. But I'm sure you won't be surprised to hear that there was not only an actual murder on our murder-mystery train, but two additional attempted murders."

A frustrated squeal echoes from somewhere in the background. "Robin Pyewacket Goodfellow! Get me down from here!"

Going a long way toward proving the theory that Pye may actually be able to hear Grams as well as me. He jumps down from the desk and disappears out of frame.

There is a considerable kerfuffle off screen, but eventually Pyewacket returns with the amber pendant dangling from his pointy-toothed mouth. It takes a moment to get it aligned properly, but at last Grams can see me.

"Oh my goodness! Your hair looks beautiful. Did you do that yourself?"

"I did. I learned from the best."

She giggles. "You certainly did. You can fill me in on the murder shenanigans when you get home. Right now, I need you to hold that phone out so I can see your getup."

I put on a private fashion show for Ghost-ma, and she hoots and hollers with delight. "That Erick Harper isn't going to be able to keep his hands off you!"

My throat tightens, and all the frivolous joy seeps out of my heart. "That's kind of why I was calling. I think I'm ready. I— Today I—"

"Oh, sweetie. We have no secrets."

"I told him I loved him."

If she weren't trapped in that pendant, she would be spinning around the room like a whirling dervish. She's squealing and wooting, and her excitement fills me with happiness and courage. "I love you too, Grams."

"And I love you, Mitzy. You and Erick deserve the most wonderful return trip in history. Knock yourself out, sweetie. Don't do anything I wouldn't do."

Barely able to get my words out between the uproarious laughter and the gasping, I choke out a response. "So that leaves a pretty wide open field, right, Isadora?"

I can picture her flashing her eyebrows and shimmying her shoulders as she says, "You only live once."

A sharp pang tightens my chest. "Silas is on his way to see his brother. I guess the guy's some kind of Latin scholar. He might have additional info that will help us with the whole amulet problem."

Grams exhales loudly. "The sooner, the better. I can't stand it in this thing. I guarantee you it's genuinely like being inside a coffin. But buried alive."

"Ew. Yuck. Don't say it like that. Silas will come through. He always does."

"Reow." Can confirm.

"See, Grams. Even Pyewacket has faith."

"I know, dear. I trusted Silas with my life once. I can do it again. But don't you worry about all this metaphysical melodrama tonight. You and your handsome sheriff have an unforgettable, possibly monumental, evening."

Now my cheeks are a red-hot crimson. "Take it easy, Grams." Before I can end the call, the compartment door opens and a Tom Ford model wearing a perfectly tailored tuxedo strikes a pose. My jaw drops and my mood soars.

"What is it, Mitzy? Is everything okay?" Grams is frantic.

"You look amazing, Erick."

He adjusts his lapel and pretends to check the time on his nonexistent watch as he throws on his gangster voice and replies, "You don't look so bad yourself, doll."

I smile and shake my head, but Grams is giggling like an idiot. "Turn the phone. Let me see him."

"Would you mind a short virtual fashion show for Grams?"

He blushes and looks at the ground. "Right. I forgot you were on the phone."

"Let me see!"

"Sorry, Erick. At this point, it's no longer optional." I turn the phone and give Grams the full head to toe.

She hoots and giggles. "I don't know how you waited this long, sweetie. Have a splendid night." And, as if on cue, Pyewacket ends the call.

Shaking my phone back and forth, I shrug. "Should we take a picture?"

He smiles warmly and beckons me with a sexy little come-hither curve of his finger.

We snap a couple pics for posterity, stash my phone in the compartment, and promenade to the Blue Heron restaurant car.

CHAPTER 18

TONIGHT'S FARE INCLUDES a fennel salad, arctic char, butternut squash with figs, onion and mushroom potato pave, and a delicious Gatsby cocktail.

Bordering on stuffed, but never too full for dessert, I compromise, and we end up *sharing* a heavenly deep-dish cran-raspberry crumble with an orange-raspberry coulis, and, of course, some freshly spun ice cream.

The Josephs stop by our table, and Bernie pats Erick heartily on the back. "You're gonna be somewhat of a legend on this train, Sheriff."

Erick chuckles. "Oh, I doubt that, Bernie. Once we all return to our normal lives, this crazy train ride will be forgotten."

"Not if I have anything to say about it."

Tootie wriggles with excitement as Erick and I look up in confusion.

"Turns out, ol' Alice wants to sell. And Tootie and I think it's time we get out of the agriculture business. Seems like the railway is just what we need."

My hands are up in the air, and my shocked expression must say it all.

Tootie grips one of my hands and squeezes it. "Bernie and I haven't had this much fun since he was on the rodeo circuit. You know, you get older and just get stuck in your ways. Sometimes you gotta shake things up. Boy, oh boy, did this locomotive shake things up."

Erick nods. "I'd have to agree with that. This train ride has taken me a lot farther than I ever thought it would."

His ulterior meaning is not lost on me, and the pink on my cheeks says as much.

Bernie swats Erick on the back one more time. "Well, I'm sure you two lovebirds would like to be alone on your last night on the train. But you keep in touch. If you ever need a romantic getaway, Bernie and Tootie are here to get you an all-expenses-paid excursion."

Erick shakes the man's hand. "Thank you, Bernie. That's awful generous of you."

I pat Tootie's hand, and we exchange a knowing

smile. Somehow Erick and I gave them a boost of energy and courage, and they gave me a wonderful sense of calm. The reassurance I needed to trust in the wonderful relationship right in front of me.

She gently extracts her hand, leans toward me, and whispers, "I know that look, dear. And you couldn't be more right." She glances toward Erick, then back to me, and winks.

As she pulls away, I place a hand on her arm. "It was you, wasn't it?"

Her face falls blank. "Me? Me what?"

For her ears only, I whisper, "You were the murderer."

She gasps.

"In the game, of course. Your wedding ring gave you away. A little glint in the darkness." No need to explain that the glint from the wedding ring story is all a ruse. I saw the ring clear as day in my clairvoyant flash. When I later caught a glimpse of the single opal surrounded by small diamonds on her left hand . . . Ta-dah. Fake mystery solved!

Her shock turns to good-natured giggles, but she nods. "Looks like you earned those tickets."

The Josephs wander off arm in arm.

Erick walks his hand across the table and turns up his palm. As I drop my hand in his, I feel the weight of doubt slide from my shoulders.

"How did you know it was Tootie?"

236 / TRIXIE SILVERTALE

Stifling a chuckle, I offer him a sly grin. "Just a hunch."

He shakes his head and rubs the back of my hand. "Would you care to take a stroll to the viewing car and watch the sunset? Or are you ready to head back to our compartment?"

"I think I'll opt for the sunset. Maybe once the train is back on track—"

He winks at me. "No pun intended, I'm sure."

"It's not my fault. There are just so many sayings that kinda seem like they have something to do with railroads. It was totally an accident."

Squeezing my hand, he offers an unconvincing nod. "I'll ask the server for a bucket of champagne and two glasses to go."

Uh oh. I better take it easy on the bubbly. There's no way I'm gonna let skanky Mitzy ruin this night.

As we pass through the cars, Erick exchanges pleasantries with the officers taking statements from passengers. He clasps my hand firmly and introduces me when appropriate.

Despite the upbeat mood and the electricity of anticipation in the air, I'd be lying if I said my elation didn't dip when we passed through the baggage car.

If Lizzie had chosen to poison me like her other victims, I wouldn't be here right now. What if I hadn't regained consciousness when I did? What if Erick hadn't found me? Yeesh! This is not the time to think about all the things that could've happened; it's time to focus my energy on what is happening now.

Wait. What is happening? "Erick, hold on."

"What is it?"

"I smell something—I think."

He smiles. "Is it luggage?"

"No. It's kind of an almond extract-y odor."

His expression turns sober. "Where?"

I'm not sure if the scent is real or psychic, but I feel like a human bloodhound. I sniff the air like an apex predator and move toward the aroma. "Here!" My nose and my finger point toward a bowling-bag size suitcase.

Erick looks around for something to pick up the case with, and spies a hand towel draped over the top of the baggage rack. He carefully places the bag on the floor near the door, where there's more light. Using the towel to clumsily grip the zipper, he opens the case.

"Bingo!" I hop and clap my hands.

"Here's that sharps disposal you were looking for earlier." He holds it up to the light and tilts it back and forth. "And, if I'm not mistaken, there's an insulin vial shoved in here too."

"And that's a hit for the Pin Cherry team!"

"Maybe a home run would sound better." Chuckling at my lack of sports knowledge, he meticulously replaces the red plastic box in the case and picks up the handle with the small towel. "Wait here. I need to hand this off to Juárez."

"Um, if you think I'm going to stand here all alone in this creepy baggage car, you are sadly mistaken, Sheriff."

"Right. Step out on the platform with me. I'll only be a minute."

He struts across the concrete expanse with his prize, and the instant that the lieutenant catches sight of him in his tuxedo, she whistles and catcalls. Erick takes it all in stride as he hands off the damning evidence.

Although, on his return trip, I can see the flame in his cheeks.

"Pookie already recovered the gun. Luckily it landed barrel down and dug into the dirt enough to keep it from bouncing wide."

"Great. I think our sleuthing duties are officially over now."

"Agreed. Where were we?"

Gripping his hand tightly, I smile at the curve of his ear, grin at the span of his shoulders, and nearly swoon at the thought of his embrace as I follow him back onto the train.

The remodeled caboose still has a seating compartment for the brakeman up top, but this level is all for show.

Sumptuous velvet drapes cascade from brass rods above etched-glass windows, and the intricate black-on-black textured wallpaper, with its subtle hints of gold, whispers of an east-Asian style.

Erick guides me to one of the two plush chairs facing roughly west and sets our iced bucket of champagne on a small marble-top table.

He pops the cork with beyond unnecessary ceremony and pours each of us a flute of bubbly. "A toast to Mitzy Moon and her inexplicable hunches." Tilting his glass toward mine, we clink the gilt edges and take a sip.

His freshly shaven face is all smiles, and his dazzling eyes gaze at me with love and admiration. If it weren't for my pesky extra senses, I wouldn't even know that a tiny piece of him was holding back. Rather than derail the evening by giving in to my obsessive snooping, I offer a toast of my own. "To Erick Harper, reluctant hero and all-around amazing guy."

We clink our glasses once more, and I take a reserved sip of my champagne.

The shimmering golden orb in front of us dips low on the horizon and shifts to a fiery pink.

"Would you care to step onto the back deck with me, Miss Moon?"

The gravelly timbre of his voice makes my heart skip a beat, and I set my champagne down too quickly. The crystalware tips onto the thick Persian carpet. "Shoot! Should I send someone to get a towel?"

Erick calmly sets down his stemware, takes my hand, and pulls me into the cool evening air. "I'm sure Bernie will forgive you."

For some reason that makes me giggle.

Slipping his arms around my waist, Erick tilts his head ever so close.

Streaks of deep purple and alpine blue spread across the sky.

His lips press against mine as the sun slips away and my eyelids flutter closed.

"All aboard!" crackles abruptly from the depot speakers.

The steam whistle blows three loud toots, announcing the end of the Scenic Railway's part in the ongoing investigation.

When I gaze into his eyes, I can read them like a book. Without bothering to ask, I take his hand in mine and lead the way back to our compartment.

The door closes and his hands gently cup my face.

His kisses always melt my insides, but the emotion in this one turns my blood to lava. His hands on my skin are so gentle and warm. I don't think I've ever felt anything like this before. The train picks up speed and I struggle with the buttons of his tuxedo jacket.

He slowly slips the strap of my dress off my shoulder and whispers quietly, "You're sure?"

"Entirely."

I'm certain Grams will forgive me just this once for not hanging up my couture.

As my fancy gown slides to the floor, the train plunges into the tunnel at full speed. The darkness envelopes our tryst, and my heart feels as though it is finally home.

A truly fade to black moment!

End of Book 13

But, the mysteries continue...
Curl up with the next book in the Mitzy Moon
Mysteries series!

A NOTE FROM TRIXIE

Finally! I can hear all you long-time series readers simultaneously shouting. Hooray for Erick and Mitzy—and another case solved! I'll keep writing them if you keep reading . . .

The best part of "living" in Pin Cherry Harbor continues to be feedback from my early readers. Thank you to my alpha readers/cheerleaders, Angel and Michael. HUGE thanks to my fantastic beta readers who continue to give me extremely useful and honest feedback: Veronica McIntyre, Margery Tipton, and Nadine Peterse-Vrijhof. And big "small town" hugs to the world's best ARC Team – Trixie's Mystery ARC Detectives!

Nobody does it better, Philip Newey. Thank you for talking me out of calling it a "preface." I'd also like to give a bucket of gratitude to Brooke for her tireless proofreading! Any errors are my own.

Shout out to Tony Hauserman for double-checking my concussion protocols.

FUN FACT: I've had two concussions in my lifetime, and one was during a broomball game!

My favorite quote from this case: "I've never met anyone who has such a codependent relationship with danger." ~ Erick to Mitzy

I'm currently writing book fifteen in the Mitzy Moon Mysteries series, and I think I may just live in Pin Cherry Harbor forever. Mitzy, Grams, and Pyewacket got into plenty of trouble in book one, *Fries and Alibis*. But I'd have to say that book three, *Wings and Broken Things*, is when most readers say the series becomes unputdownable.

I hope you'll continue to hang out with us.

Trixie Silvertale (April 2021)

Mitzy Moon Mysteries #14

A dangerous tornado. A clever crime. Can this psychic sleuth sift through the rubble to find a murder?

Mitzy Moon longs to embrace the warmth of summer at a community-wide celebration. Enjoying a midsummer sailboat regatta, strawberry cake, and bonfires on the beach sounds divine. But when dark skies unleash a super-storm, the festivities turn deadly . . .

While everyone pitches in to rescue stranded friends and neighbors from the wreckage, Mitzy senses evil in the debris. Her entitled feline is missing and the handsome sheriff is in no mood for her hunches. But she refuses to buy into his black cloud of skepticism, because she's sure one of the bodies didn't die of natural causes.

Can Mitzy catch a killer before the clues are washed away?

Castaways and Longer Days is the fourteenth book in the hilarious paranormal cozy mystery series, Mitzy Moon Mysteries. If you like snarky heroines, supernatural misfits, and a splash of romance, then you'll love Trixie Silvertale's twisty whodunit.

Buy *Castaways and Longer Days* to sink an assassin today!

Grab yours here!
readerlinks.com/l/5212008

Scan this QR Code with the camera on your phone. You'll be taken right to the next case!

SPECIAL INVITATION . . .

Come visit Pin Cherry Harbor!

Get access to the Exclusive Mitzy Moon Mysteries character quiz – free!

Find out which character you are in Pin Cherry Harbor and see if you have what it takes to be part of Mitzy's gang.

This quiz is only available to members of the Paranormal Cozy Club, Trixie Silvertale's reader group.

Visit the link below to join the club and get access to the quiz:

Join Trixie's Club
https://trixiesilvertale.com/paranormal-cozy-club/

Once you're in the Club, you'll also be the first to receive updates from Pin Cherry Harbor and access to giveaways, new release announcements, behind-the-scenes secrets, and much more!

Scan this QR Code with the camera on your phone. You'll be taken right to the page to join the Club!

THANK YOU!

Trying out a new book is always a risk and I'm thankful that you rolled the dice with Mitzy Moon. If you loved the book, the sweetest thing you can do (*even sweeter than pin cherry pie à la mode*) is to leave a review so that other readers will take a chance on Mitzy and the gang.

Don't feel you have to write a book report. A brief comment like, "Can't wait to read the next book in this series!" will help potential readers make their choice.

Leave a quick review HERE
https://readerlinks.com/l/1671608
★★★★★

Thank you kindly, and I'll see you in Pin Cherry Harbor!

ALSO BY TRIXIE SILVERTALE

Mitzy Moon Mysteries
Paranormal Cozy Mysteries

Fries and Alibis

Tattoos and Clues

Wings and Broken Things

Sparks and Landmarks

Charms and Firearms

Bars and Boxcars

Swords and Fallen Lords

Wakes and High Stakes

Tracks and Flashbacks

Lies and Pumpkin Pies

Hopes and Slippery Slopes

Hearts and Dark Arts

Dames and Deadly Games

Castaways and Longer Days

Schemes and Bad Dreams

Carols and Yule Perils

Dangers and Empty Mangers

Heists and Poltergeists

Blades and Bridesmaids

Scones and Tombstones

Vandals and Yule Scandals

Harper and Moon Investigations
Paranormal Cozy Mysteries

Ropes and Last Hopes

Bells and Bombshells

Rodeo Clowns and Shakedowns

Stiffs and Petroglyphs

Fatal Wines and Valentines

April Curses and May Hearses

Wheels and Dirty Deals

Scripts and Empty Crypts

Christmas Catastrophe Mysteries
Culinary Cozy Mysteries

Peppermint Cookie Murder

Apple Dumpling Murder

Linzer Cookie Murder

Chocolate Crinkle Cookie Murder

...more to come!

MAGICAL RENAISSANCE FAIRE MYSTERIES

Explore the world of Coriander the Conjurer. A fortune-telling fairy with a heart of gold!

Book 1:

All Swell That Ends Spell – A dubious festival. A fatal swim. Can this fortune-telling fairy herald the true killer?

Book 2:

Fairy Wives of Windsor – A jolly Faire. A shocking murder. Can this furtive fairy outsmart the killer?

Book 3:

Double Double Royal Trouble – When a treat-peddling witch is found dead, will this cursed faire crumble?

Join Sydney Coleman and her unruly ghosts, as they solve mysteries in a truly haunted mansion!

Book 1: **Moonlight and Mischief** – She's desperate for a fresh start, but is a mansion on sale too good to be true?

Book 2: **Moonlight and Magic** – A haunted Halloween tour seem like the perfect plan, until there's murder...

Book 3: ***Moonlight and Mayhem*** – An unwelcome visitor. A surprising past. Will her fire sale end in smoke?

ABOUT THE AUTHOR

USA TODAY Bestselling author Trixie Silvertale grew up reading an endless supply of Lilian Jackson Braun, Hardy Boys, and Nancy Drew novels. She loves the amateur sleuths in cozy mysteries and obsesses about all things paranormal. Those two passions unite in all her cozy mysteries, and she's thrilled to write them and share them with you.

When she's not consumed by writing, she bakes to fuel her creative engine and pulls weeds in her herb garden to clear her head (*and sometimes she pulls out her hair, but mostly weeds*).

Greetings are welcome:
trixie@trixiesilvertale.com

f facebook.com/TrixieSilvertale

instagram.com/trixiesilvertale

BB bookbub.com/authors/trixie-silvertale

www.ingramcontent.com/pod-product-compliance
Lightning Source LLC
Chambersburg PA
CBHW021957170626
46808CB00001B/190